Out of Sight...
Out of Murder

A Mystery Comedy

by Fred Carmichael

SAMUEL FRENCH
FOUNDED 1830
New York Hollywood London Toronto
SAMUELFRENCH.COM

Out Of Sight ... Out Of Murder
by Fred Carmichael

Premier Performance By The Valley Players,
Waitsfield, Vermont.

Staged by Curtis Wright

(in order of appearance)

Peter Knight...........................Huck Davies
Minna ....Joann Flanagan
Lydia.................................Kimberly Cruz
Cogburn ....Mitchell Kontoff
Kay Kelsey ....Nancy Cohen
Fiona ....Wendy Cohen
Addie................................Robin Grinnel
Dick Stanton ....Bill McMullin
Jordan Dillingham......................Jake Brickman

SCENE
The living room of an old house in Vermont.

TIME

ACT ONE
A late summer afternoon. The present.

ACT TWO
scene 1
Later that day. Evening.

scene 2
A short time later.

Produced by Barbara Wright and Ronald Court
Setting Designed by Donald Hirsch

3

ACT ONE

Out Of Sight ... Out Of Murder
by
Fred Carmichael

SET: *(The action of the play takes place in the living room of a very old mansion in Vermont. Not a typical Vermont house, the room looks more like the setting for a Victorian mystery. Up center a stairway leads to the upstairs of the house. There is a landing a few steps up and then the exit to the hallway. Above the stairs there is a passage leading to the off-stage library. To the right a hall leads off to the front door. A short wall right stage has built-in bookshelves, down right is a typing table with a typewriter on it with a half-typed sheet of paper in it. Just above this is a desk with a swivel chair to the right stage of it so the chair can be used at the desk or the typing table. The left wall jogs onstage a few feet and then there is the opening for the up center getaway and stairs. The left wall has an archway opening leading to the dining room and kitchen. Below this is a large fireplace with no fire laid, it being*

5

summer. Above the fireplace is a large armchair with a small table to its left. A small straight chair is in the down left corner. Center stage is a sofa with pillows and above it is a table. Onstage of the desk, which runs perpendicular to the audience, is a backless, padded bench. A bell cord to summon the servants is upstage of the dining room arch. The appearance of the room is of heavy molding, dark wood and over-hanging shadows.)

(Typing is heard. The curtain rises to show PETER KNIGHT at the typewriter. PETER is probably in his mid-thirties, a man who is very harried at the moment. He is dressed casually in shirt and slacks. The typewriter keys stick.)

PETER.
PETER. What good did Physics do me? I should have taken a typing course. *(He undoes the stuck keys and resumes typing. The phone rings.) (into phone)* Yes ... Fine, Jason, just fine ... *(looking around at room)* Yes, I would say it is gloomy. I would say just that... How do I know if the Vermont air is pure? You think I've been out in it? You gave me the deadline ... Oh, no! ... Now look, Alan, I know an agent is supposed to push his client, but you're sending me into a sanitarium ... OK, what's the name? *(Writes it down.)* Phil Smith ... I'll have Minna meet the bus. What's the time?... Got it ... Minna? ... Oh, Alan, you'd be consumed with jealousy. She's about twenty, long blonde hair, and a figure an eight would be jealous of. *(MINNA comes in up center. She is a hefty and strong lady used to working on the farm, but she is fun to be with and has an intense manner about her. She wears a cotton house dress.)* You should see her in a bikini. Good morning, Minna.

MINNA. Ayah, hope so.

PETER. *(into phone)* Yes .. *(glances at MINNA)* Oh, about 36 - 24 - 35. *(to MINNA)* Those are my lottery numbers.

MINNA. Ayah.

PETER. *(into phone)* Yes, Alan, I'll make your deadline if your Phil Smith can take decent dictation. Now let me get to work. *(hangs up)*

MINNA. *(goes to left of desk)* You spend a lot of time on the telephone.

PETER. That was my agent. He'll charge it to me and then I'll make it deductible so Uncle Sam pays for it. What can I do for you, Minna?

MINNA. Question is what I can do for you. You pay me.

PETER. The real estate agent pays you.

MINNA. And you pay the rent. Same thing.

PETER. I don't think I'm in need, Minna. Possibly buckets if the roof leaks. There is a storm coming on.

MINNA. Roof's sound as a tractor seat.

PETER. That's good?

MINNA. Ayah. *(Goes to table above sofa and picks up magazines and straightens the pile.)* Never got no complaints about leaks. Other things though. Mice, flies, rottin' boards and, of course, ghosts.

PETER. *(goes to MINNA)* Mice and flies I can believe but not ghosts.

MINNA. It's the wind whistlin' through the upstairs hall. That's what it is.

PETER. I thought it might be old Norman Napier.

MINNA. *(crosses above desk to typing table)* Lands sakes, he's passed over. I don't hold with people comin' back. Once you've left it's one way, not round trip.

PETER. My sentiments exactly.

MINNA. *(Pointing to paper in typewriter.)* What you're typin', that goin, to be a book or what?

PETER. *(goes to right of sofa)* I hope a book and not a "what".

MINNA. Will it be on the TV?

PETER. *(sits on sofa)* One can always hope.

MINNA. *(goes to right of desk)* I like TV. Saves time. Instead of readin' "She says", you can just watch her sayin' it.

PETER. The redeeming grace is no commercials.

MINNA. *(sits on the bench)* Ayah. Pearly likes the ones for beer. Reminds him to open a can.

PETER. How is your husband doing?

MINNA. Damned fool. Spends all his time fixin' everyone else's house and pays no attention to ours. I been hintin' that them cellar stairs was rottin' away. Why, I haven't used the third from the top since last time the sap was runnin'.

PETER. And you didn't tell him?

MINNA. Lands, I wouldn't tell him a thing. He'll be outta the cast come Tuesday. He probably would have tended to you better'n me.

PETER. You've been a great help, Minna.

MINNA. *(crosses to him)* Folks come up here and rent this place, they don't know nothin' about it. Got to tell 'em all the little odd things about it, y'know. Where to check the hot-water tank, where the fuse box is, how to jiggle the handle on the toilet upstairs after you flush.

PETER. I'm just glad it flushes. When my agent got this place I had visions of an outdoor john and kerosene lamps.

MINNA. *(goes to desk looking toward typewriter)* Why'd he get this for you anyways? Bad luck for authors, this is.

PETER. Because of Norman Napier?

MINNA. Ayah.

PETER. *(crosses to her)* Maybe he's the lucky one. He doesn't have to worry about deadlines any more.

MINNA. Don't have to worry about nothin' no more. *(points to typewriter table)* Right there was where I found him.

PETER. At his typewriter. How appropriate.

MINNA. Nice to go while you're at work, I reckon. I'll just keel over into my johnny-cake.

PETER. *(crosses to fireplace)* If Napier hadn't died here I wouldn't be here. Did you ever think of that?

MINNA. Can't say I did.

PETER. An author dies here of mysterious circumstances -

MINNA. *(moves in center)* Nothin' mysterious. He just died.

PETER. But why?

MINNA. Heart stopped pumpin'.

PETER. Exactly, but they couldn't find a cause. He just died. It got a lot of publicity for him when he didn't need it. He was right at the top of his popularity.

MINNA. You at the top?

PETER. *(sits in chair left)* Minna, you always ask the wrong things.

MINNA. Believe in speakin' my mind.

PETER. I was at the top several years ago but now I need a good mystery so what better place to write it than here?

MINNA. *(sits on the sofa)* If your heart don't stop.

PETER. It's all my agent's idea. "Write a good murder mystery in that mausoleum where Napier died," he said. "Great publicity." He even gave me a title. "Death of an Author".

MINNA. Kinda catchy.

PETER. It's working. Did you see this week's *Newsweek?*

MINNA. Must have missed that.

PETER. *(gets it from table above sofa)* But I still can't get a handle on it. *(looks for his article)* I've started it though. Have a collection of characters coming in here and - *(finds the article and shows it to her over the back of the sofa)* Here it is.

MINNA. Why, that's you, ain't it?

PETER. Yes.

MINNA. You look real intelligent there.

PETER. *(puts magazine back and goes down by left of sofa)* I wish I was there. That's taken in Southampton.

MINNA. That's in England.

PETER. This one's on Long Island. *(sits on sofa)* I have an ultra-modern house there looking right out over the ocean.

MINNA. And you left it?

PETER. I rented it. Needed the money. Royalties are not what they used to be and the place is hocked up to its skylight.

MINNA. Maybe you should think of gettin' a real job.

PETER. This is a real job.

MINNA. I mean like work, somethin' by the hour.

PETER. But I'm a writer.

MINNA. Then you should be writin' instead of talkin'.

PETER. I'm too scared to write.

MINNA. What you scared of?

PETER. Well, to tell the truth, I don't know where I'm headed. I've gotten as far as bringing some characters in but I'm not quite sure where the mystery is going.

MINNA. This is a perfect place for a murder all right.

PETER. *(paces over to desk)* But it is hardly a typical Vermont house. This belongs to Edgar Allen Poe.

MINNA. Not Poe. Pocock.

PETER. What?

MINNA. Abner Pocock had this place built back in the last century. *(PETER sits on the bench.)* He wanted a showplace when he spent the summers here. T'ain't another house like it in the whole county. Cost a bundle, too. *(goes to PETER)* Now-a-days you can't even afford to heat it. That's why no one rents it in the winters. Not even skiiers and, Lord knows, they'll rent anything. The Cutlers rented their little two bedroom Cape and you know how many skiiers crammed in there?

PETER. More than four?

MINNA. Twenty-three. They was sleepin' everywhere. Wouldn't be surprised if they find one in the freezer. *(goes up center)* Well, I gotta make my legs start movin'. You want anythin' down to the store?

PETER. *(goes to her)* You've kept me well supplied, Minna. There is one thing, though.

MINNA. Ayah.

PETER. Could you meet the morning bus from the city?

MINNA. The ten twenty-five?

PETER. And pick up a Phil Smith. He's going to be my secretary, take dictation and all that. I'm sure you'll recognize him. He's bound to be a short, plump man with owl spectacles. No, that's mean. He's probably a very nice-looking out of work actor.

MINNA. And he's bound to be the only one gettin' off the bus.

PETER. That's true enough.

MINNA. *(starts out)* I'll stop in later with the paper.

PETER. I'm sure the Burlington Free Press is fine, but could you bring the New York Times this time?

MINNA. Everyone to his own taste as the old lady said when she kissed the cow.

PETER. *(smiles)* Thanks, Minna.

MINNA. And don't forget to jiggle the upstairs toilet. *(She goes off up right.)*

PETER. *(as he sees her out)* That is uppermost in my mind. *(He comes back, sits at typewriter and thinks a moment. reads over what he has written)* "... as the thunder echoes throughout the mountains." *(thunder sound in distance)* Oh, that's all I need. *(reads more)* "It was as if the old house was preparing for murder. But at that moment all was calm and tranquil. The countryside was growing darker." No. *(speaks as he types)* "... was growing dimmer as if fortelling the events of the grusome evening ahead. Oblivious of the storm's warning, Lydia came to the top of the stairs."*(LYDIA appears on the landing. She is an attractive woman in her forties, dressed and groomed beautifully. She is sophisticated, brittle, and caustic but with a good sense of humor. PETER doesn't see her.)* "She is an exquisite creature.

LYDIA. That's obvious.

PETER. "Lydia is probably forty-two years old."

LYDIA. Why am I always over forty?

PETER. "But she carries it well."

LYDIA. Make-up does wonders.

PETER. "Only a close inspection would reveal her true age and many men have had the advantage of that close inspection." *(looks up)* I like that.

LYDIA. So do I.

PETER. *(resumes typing)* "As usual, she is dressed with impeccable taste."

LYDIA. That's a relief.

PETER. "A green scarf is wound round her throat."

LYDIA. Blue. Couldn't I have blue?

PETER. *(rereads)* "a green scarf ..."

LYDIA. Oh, hell. *(exits off landing)*

PETER. *(thinks to himself)* That could be used in a murder, of course. Scarves are always handy. A quick twist and it's all over.

LYDIA. *(comes back onto landing tying a green scarf around her neck)* I hope you're satisfied. Green.

PETER. *(types)* "She comes downstairs." *(She does.)* "There is an ominous roll of thunder." *(Thunder rumbles. LYDIA shivers.)* "It sends a shiver through her."

LYDIA. Thunder makes me nervous.

PETER. "She paces the room nervously."

LYDIA. *(She paces to fireplace and back below sofa.)* I'm going to get murdered. I know it. I always do.

PETER. "She sits on the sofa trying to calm her nerves." *(She does.)* "She picks up a magazine."

LYDIA. *(gets a copy of THE READER'S DIGEST from table above sofa)* The Readers Digest? Why can't I ever read anything uncondensed?

PETER. "There is another clap of thunder." *(thunder)* "Lydia rises in alarm." *(She does.)*

LYDIA. You don't have to write that. I'd do it anyway.

PETER. "She hears footsteps coming from the kitchen into the dining room." *(sound of footsteps off left)* "Every nerve in her body is alert and tingling."

LYDIA. Don't murder me yet. I just got here.

PETER. "The footsteps come closer and closer and ..."

(Lights go out. BLACKOUT. Sound of rain can be heard intermittently from now on, but it is mainly audible the few times the front door is opened. LIGHTNING FLASH.)

PETER. Oh, hell! This wouldn't happen in Southampton. I mustn't panic. The flashlight's here in the desk somewhere. Somewhere, but where? Here it is. *(PETER lights the flashlight he has gotten from desk drawer.)* There we are. I wonder if it's this house or the whole town.

LYDIA. *(from the darkness)* Just this house, darling.

PETER. Who said that?

LYDIA. I did.

PETER. *(flashlight on her face)* Who are - how did you get in here? What's going on?

LYDIA. The lightning blew something-or-other.

PETER. But who are you?

LYDIA. Lydia.

PETER. Lydia?

LYDIA. *(moves to him)* Don't you recognize me? The green scarf and all that? I did so want to keep the blue.

PETER. You mean you're Lydia - my Lydia?

LYDIA. *(sits on the bench leaning towards him)* All yours, darling.

PETER. The lightning. I've been struck by lightning, that's it. Call an ambulance, the rescue squad. *(picks up phone on desk)* They must have a rescue squad.

LYDIA. The phone's out. It always is.

PETER. *(trying to get a dial tone)* You're right. *(hangs up)* Now suppose you tell me.what this is all about?

LYDIA. Suppose you tell me. You're the author.

PETER. I am hallucinating, but I don't take drugs, I don't even take aspirin that's extra-strength. *(lights flicker)*

LYDIA. Goody. The light's are coming back.

PETER. I want to know what you are doing here. *(lights come on and stay on)*

LYDIA. There we are. Now you can put that beastly torch out, there's a good boy. I must say you're better looking than most I've worked for. A trifle sallow, perhaps, but some Vermont sunshine will take care of that.

PETER. *(flashlight in desk drawer)* Let's start all over. Who are you?

LYDIA. Lydia   Whatever-you-decided.   Dillingham, wasn't it? But then you hadn't really made up your mind.

PETER. But Lydia Dillingham is - she isn't real - she's in there. *(points to typewriter)*

LYDIA. No, dear, up there in your head. *(rises and turns a circle for him to admire her)* Do I look like you expected? You didn't describe every last detail yet. I hope you like the hair. Do you?

PETER. It's very fetching.

LYDIA. Thank you. Now tell me, am I going to get murdered? I don't particularly want to be but I usually am.

PETER. I've fallen asleep. I am dreaming and that's why you're here.

LYDIA. *(sits on sofa and relaxes back)* That's not quite it. I am Lydia, though, do you believe that for starters?

PETER. I'll have to. You look like her, you sound like her, but -

LYDIA. Good. You created me and here I am. Aren't you happy to see me?

PETER. *(crosses center)* I never expected to meet you - in the flesh if that's what you're in.

LYDIA. It's all been a lucky happenstance. You were thinking and writing and the lightning came exactly at the right moment and zingo, here I am. It doesn't happen very often.

PETER. But it has happened before?

LYDIA. Occasionally when all the elements meet at the right moment. We're always around, you know, the people you think up. We're in your head running about doing your bidding. It's probably my running around in high heels that gives you headaches.

PETER. I suppose you think that's amusing?

LYDIA. You did give me a sense of humor.

PETER. *(crosses to fireplace)* Well, it's warped.

LYDIA. Then it's your fault.

PETER. How long are you going to be around?

LYDIA. As long as you need us to write your story.

PETER. *(turns to her)* You said "us". There are others here?

LYDIA. Of course, all your characters.

PETER. I'm like Pirandello. I've got six characters in search of me.

LYDIA. Pirandello's a bore. I worked for him once.

PETER. You mean like this?

LYDIA. No, darling. He didn't bring us to life. We stayed in his head. Gloomy place. *(rises and goes to PETER)* Peter - may I call you Peter since we know each other so well?

PETER. Why not?

LYDIA. Peter, might I have a drink?

PETER. You can drink? You're not just ectoplasm or something?

LYDIA. When we get released we can do everything. *(leans closer to him)* Everything.

PETER. I'll get that drink. *(starts to go out dining room arch)*

LYDIA. No, you don't have to. Pull the bell cord. There. *(points to bell cord above dining room arch)*

PETER. *(pulls the cord)* I don't believe it. You're telling me the butler will come?

LYDIA. *(moves away center)* It's his duty.

PETER. What's his name? I changed it last night. It was -
Cogburn.

LYDIA. He's very good at butlers, been playing them for
centuries.

COGBURN. *(Enters from dining room. He is older than the
others and is, in every sense, the typical butler, proper, quiet,
unemotional. He knows his job to perfection and relishes it. He is
dressed in a butler's outfit. He comes to behind PETER'S back.)*
You rang, sir?

PETER. *(Startled, he turns.)* Oh, my God!

COGBURN. No, sir. I'm Cogburn.

LYDIA. I rang. Cogburn, could you get me a nice Scotch
and water? I don't suppose there is any Chivas Regal
out there?

PETER. No.

COGBURN. Certainly, Madame. For you, sir?

PETER. *(at wit's end)* Why the hell not?

COGBURN. Very good, sir. *(exits)*

LYDIA. He's a dear.

PETER. How did the Chivas Regal get here?

LYDIA. Cogburn always brings the best. Evidently you
hadn't written what kind of a liquor supply was here.

PETER. I hope I did the same with the food.

LYDIA. *(crosses to him)* Food! Oh, Peter, to eat again. How
marvelous.

PETER. How long since you've had a meal?

LYDIA. *(sits on right end of sofa)* Let's see now. There was
that dreadful Mickey Spillane thing. I didn't eat there, of
course. I spent most of my time in bed. Then there was -
do you know, Peter, I can't remember when I ate my
last meal.

PETER. *(sits next to her)* That's quite a diet.

LYDIA. *(leans back on sofa)* A good figure is one of my specialties.

PETER. Then, for now, you are real? You and Cogburn are solid flesh?

LYDIA. Very solid, Peter, and moulded just right.

PETER. When the Author's Guild hears about this -

LYDIA. No fair, Peter, You can't exploit us so don't go calling 60 MINUTES.

PETER. Who has time? I am on a deadline to finish my book.

LYDIA. That's why we're here. We're only real to you.

PETER. Who would believe this?

LYDIA. If you try to tell anyone, you'll only end up in a sanitarium. It's happened before.

COGBURN. *(enters with two highballs on a tray; goes above sofa to LYDIA)* I hope these will be satisfactory, sir.

PETER. I imagine they will be.

LYDIA. *(takes her drink)* Cogburn.

COGBURN. Yes, Madame.

LYDIA. You don't have to be formal. We're set free. This dear author has released us.

COGBURN. *(with his usual calm)* I know. I'm very excited.

PETER. You don't seem it.

COGBURN. *(goes above sofa to give PETER his drink)* Butlers are butlers. Our excitement is within.

LYDIA. Come on, relax. Make yourself a drink and join us.

COGBURN. *(shocked)* Oh, Madame.

LYDIA. We're all in the same boat. Sit down, have a smoke.

COGBURN. I couldn't sit in here. *(goes to dining room and turns)* But if I might, I'll take a small libation in the pantry.

PETER. Enjoy yourself, Cogburn.

COGBURN. Thank you, sir. *(exits)*

LYDIA. He'll loosen up when he gets used to being free.

PETER. Does he have to stay in the character I invented for him?

LYDIA. We all have our specialties. There are all sorts of butlers, proper ones, lower class ones, trainees, even those who rob their employers blind. Cogburn is one of the top sophisticates, but he really excells in murder mysteries. He used to work so much he was hardly ever at home.

PETER. Where is home?

LYDIA. Where we come from.

PETER. Which is where?

LYDIA. Shh! There are some things it's unwise to talk about. *(doorbell rings)*

PETER. *(rises)*Someone's here. How can I explain you?

LYDIA. You don't have to. They won't be able to see us.

PETER. But your drink? What about that? Will it just float around in the air?

LYDIA. I won't touch my glass in the presence of company.

PETER. And I'll just ignore you?

LYDIA. That's right, but have you thought it might be one of us at the door?

PETER. *(crosses up to right of arch)* Good Lord, which one?

COGBURN. *(enters)* There is a visitor, sir. Shall I answer it?

PETER. I guess so.

COGBURN. Very well, sir. *(turns back before leaving)* I do hope it isn't an unexpected guest, sir. They always cause such mayhem. *(exits off right)*

LYDIA. *(rises)* I think I'll go up and finish unpacking. I know who that must be. *(goes up the stairs)*

PETER. I can't entertain anyone else. I have to work.

LYDIA. *(on landing with her drink)* But, Peter, isn't it time for the beautiful ingenue to enter all rain soaked and fragile looking?

PETER. You must mean Kay? I called her Kay.

LYDIA. That's the one. Those ingenues are always so sweet and boring.

PETER. *(goes below stairs)* She might be very nice.

LYDIA. She'll come in saying - *(imitating ingenue)* "Oh, I'm so wet. I must look a fright." *(stops imitating)* Just you wait and see. *(exits upstairs)*

COGBURN. *(comes in up center leaving room for the guest below him)* Right this way, Miss.

(KAY enters   She is the typical ingenue, sweet, ingenuous, and trusting. She is lovely looking and wears a raincoat and carries a small suitcase.)

Oh, I'm so wet. I must look a fright.

COGBURN. Allow me to take your coat, Miss.

KAY. Thank you. *(COGBURN takes her coat and goes off up right.)*

PETER. How do you do. I'm Peter Knight.

KAY. I know. I wish you hadn't brought me here in the rain. It makes such a bad impression.

PETER. I didn't mean to bring you here at all.

KAY. Well, that's a nice greeting, I must say. I go to all this trouble, not that I had any choice in the matter, of course, and then you're not glad to see me.

PETER. Of course I'm glad. It's just that you're so unexpected.

KAY. *(laughs and goes by the desk)* No, I'm not the unexpected guest. I never am. I'm the ingenue. Everyone falls in love with me and some even try to kill me, but I am never the unexpected guest.

PETER. *(goes to her)* But you don't get killed, do you?

KAY. *(moves below typewriter and looks at paper in it)* Silly man. What kind of mystery would it make if the ingenue got killed just as the hero was about to save her? You know better than that.

COGBURN. *(reappears U C)* May I get you a drink, Miss?

ANN KAY. *(warning him)* Cogburn -

COGBURN. Sorry, Miss. *(comes down a few steps)* How about a cup of nice hot tea?

KAY. *(goes below PETER to COGBURN)* Perfect. Thank you. You're very sweet.

COGBURN. *(goes out dining room)* Thank you, Miss.

KAY. I always find everyone very sweet. Isn't that sickening?

PETER. I rather like it.

KAY. It palls on one after awhile. *(goes below sofa)* Shall we sit down and wait?

PETER. For the tea, you mean?

KAY. For the tea and midnight.

PETER. *(moves into sofa R)* What happens at midnight?

KAY. *(sits on L side of sofa)* Really, Peter, you ought to know. It's your story. I sometimes wish things would happen at eleven-forty or even at one o'clock but no. You authors always stick to midnight like glue.

PETER. Readers expect it.

KAY. I suppose they do. Well, now, aren't you surprised to see us?

PETER. That is an understatement.

KAY. It's going to be such fun being free for a bit. Oh, we'll stick to your story. We have to, but we can enjoy ourselves a bit.

PETER. I do hope you have a good time.

KAY. My only wish is that I can have a nice hot bath with loads of fragrant bubbles in it.

PETER. I'll try to arrange it.

KAY. There is a tub and hot water, isn't there? This place looks rather like the House of Usher.

PETER. It has all the modern conveniences.

KAY. May I ask a rather impertinent question?

PETER. Be my guest.

KAY. Why did you have to make your story happen here? There are lots of other nicer places. The Riviera, for instance. I always have a good time there. The sun, the gambling -

PETER. The topless beaches.

KAY. Not for me. I'm the ingenue.

PETER. Wishful thinking.

KAY. You are nice, Peter.

PETER. Thank you.

KAY. Now tell me. Why here?

PETER. It's all due to publicity. Norman Napier died here.

KAY. I never liked him. I worked in his head once for that thing about the corpse - yes, THE CORPSE WITH ONE SHOE. He was much too graphic.

PETER. Napier died here under rather peculiar circumstances.

KAY. *(laughs)* You authors love that, don't you?

PETER. What?

KAY. That phrase "under peculiar circumstances". It explains a great deal and nothing at the same time.

PETER. You're clever for an ingenue.

KAY. Why does everyone think we have to be so dumb?

PETER. Anyway, my agent thought it would be good to do a murder mystery set right here in the old house where Napier died. I'm supposed to use all the stock characters of the twenties but give them a modern twist.

KAY. It might make a TV movie but, as a book - well, I doubt it will even be a Book of the Month Club alternate.

COGBURN. *(enters from dining room with cup of tea, sugar bowl, and spoon on a tray)* I believe you take your tea with one sugar?

KAY. Good for you, Cogburn. *(He holds tray while she puts in one spoonful of sugar.)* You remembered.

COGBURN. Yes, Miss.

KAY. Whenever we work together he gives me my one sugar. If the author specifies something else, of course, I have to follow it. *(to COGBURN)* Remember that dreadful time I had that movie script to do?

COGBURN. THE BURNT CAMELIA? Oh, yes, Miss.

KAY. The author made me take four sugars and cream.

COGBURN. And the cream was poisoned.

KAY. I had that stomach pump scene in the hospital. There aren't any hospitals in this, are there?

PETER. Not so far.

KAY. Thank you, Cogburn. Isn't it fun being free for once?

COGBURN. Yes, Miss. *(as he exits)* Perhaps after dinner, I'll relax and have a good laugh.

KAY. He's a dear. Always right there when you need him.

PETER. He could have inspired Wodehouse to write Jeeves.

KAY. He did. *(sips tea)* This is good. There, you see what I mean about Cogburn. This wasn't made with a flow-through tea bag. It's genuine orange pekoe with a touch of camomile.

PETER. I'm glad I thought him up.

KAY. I suppose it's all for the best you have the mystery set here. If it wasn't, we wouldn't have been set free. There was a bolt of lightning, I assume?

PETER. Rather a big one.

KAY. That always does it. If the story takes place where it's written and there's a good shot of lightning, we're in. Or rather out.

PETER. Out of where?

KAY. Out of - you know, that's strange. *(rises and puts her* cup on table above sofa) I was about to tell you, but now it's all gotten fuzzy. I live in a nice place, I know that, and I report to a large room and wait to be called along with hundreds of others.

PETER. Other characters?

KAY. *(moves to R of sofa)* Every conceivable kind of person from mad rapists to happy philanthropists. When an author dreams us up in his mind, we go off till the story's finished. That's all I can remember.

PETER. *(rises and goes to her)* How long have you been there?

KAY. *(goes below him to the fireplace)* Oh, Peter, let's not get into time. It's all so relative.

PETER. Silly question, I guess.

KAY. *(turns)* Tell me about yourself. Are you happy?

PETER. *(crosses to her)* I guess so. I never stop to think about it unless I'm unhappy.

KAY. Are you married?

PETER. No. You?

KAY. *(goes to her tea on the table and sips)* I don't remember having marriages back there. But I do know when I work I'm always engaged. Sometimes my fiance is the murdered but then there's always some other nice young man around to save me, especially if I'm an heiress. That's always messy because everyone wants to marry me for my money.

PETER. I was thinking of making you an heiress in this.

KAY. You're forgiven. *(goes to him)* You're a very nice author, Peter. We don't get to talk to many of them but we do know what goes on in their heads. If I were a real person, I'd want to be engaged to someone just like you.

PETER. It would be nice to dream up your own girl and have her a real person.

KAY. Would she be like me?

PETER. I guess she would. I made you up.

KAY. Thank you for that. I wish I could stay.

PETER. So do I.

KAY. *(sits in chair L.)* But after midnight things will start popping and who knows what will happen.

PETER. Why do you keep harping on midnight?

KAY. The will. You planned to have it read at midnight.

PETER. *(crosses R.)* It was just an idea.

KAY. That's all we need. You planned it so we have to do it. Rather hackneyed, isn't it?

PETER. This is an old-time plot with new twists so there is a will read at midnight. *(goes above bench)* But we don't have to if you don't want to.

KAY. But we do, Peter. It's - well, it's ordained I guess you'd say. Who else will be here for the reading?

PETER. God knows. This has gotten out of hand. Maybe I should go upstairs and check the rooms to see who's here.

(FIONA BABCOCK comes onto the landing. She is the character lady and fits the part exactly. She is dressed severly with her hair tied back in a bun. She is well into her fifties or sixties and knows everyone else is wrong. She carries a knitting bag.)

FIONA. I am here, Mr. Knight and I am very distraught. *(marches down the stairs)*

PETER. *(shocked at another one appearing)* You're distraught? I'm hysterical.

KAY. *(whispers to him)* The old character lady.

PETER. I'm sorry, Miss - Mrs?

FIONA. Miss Fiona Babcock. You ought to know. You thought me up. *(comes to the R. of sofa)* But you didn't take enough time to think up a decent room for me. It's too bright. That wallpaper, roses everywhere. And the bed is lumpy and, Heaven forbid, there is a connecting bath to the next room and the water runs unless you jiggle the toilet handle.

PETER. Perhaps I could rethink your room.

FIONA. It's too late for that. We're free now and we're stuck with our accommodations. Hello, Kay.

KAY. I didn't know you were on call for this story.

FIONA. That author seems to have dug up all the old characters so here I am complete with knitting. *(holds up her knitting bag)* And, as usual, I am not content. You, I suppose are deliriously ecstatic?

KAY. I am rather.

FIONA. I've never worked with you when you weren't. Now, Mr. Knight, what shall we do?

PETER. What can we do?

FIONA. Nothing, that's what. *(crosses below sofa)* Nothing can ever be done. I have been upset for more stories than you'll ever write. *(sits on sofa)* That Christie woman, Agatha, she always uses me and never lets me get what I want, a little comfortable corner to call my own. On top of that, she usually murders me by the fourth chapter.

PETER. I'll do whatever -

FIONA. And another thing.

PETER. Yes.

FIONA. Can you manage to control that hysterical maid up there?

PETER. What maid?

FIONA. That incompetent idiot trying to unpack my things.

KAY. *(rises laughing)* It can't be, but it must be. Is it Addie?

FIONA. Naturally. That child haunts me.

PETER. Who is Addie?

FIONA. You named her. You brought her here.

PETER. *(crosses above sofa to R.)* I remember thinking there should be the usual maid but I hadn't really decided what kind.

FIONA. Oh, yes, you had, Mr. Knight. You authors have some stupid child rushing about all the time. Sometimes for humor, sometimes just to have another person to murder off. But they're always opposed to everything I stand for. Always. I'm sure she is unmarried and pregnant.

PETER. I wouldn't know. I -

FIONA. Then the subconscious knows. You people are preoccupied with sex. I believe that -

KAY. *(crosses down L.)* Please, Fiona, don't get started on one of your diatribes on purity. We all know how you feel. You've said it often enough. *(sits on chair down L.)*

FIONA. It bears repeating. As an author, Mr. Knight, perhaps you will tell me why you always have sexy young things prancing through your pages?

PETER. Well, I guess it's -

FIONA. Yes.

PETER. It's just that it sells well. We do have to appeal to the public.

FIONA. Money. That's all you people ever think of.

PETER. I suppose you don't need it in your - should I call it a profession?

FIONA. Money is of no importance to me.

PETER. If you had to go out and earn your own living it would be. You get everything handed to you on a silver platter. Why should you care what sells and what doesn't? I think you are very selfish. *(sits on the bench)*

FIONA. Well!

KAY. *(rises and goes to PETER)* Don't blame her too much, Peter. That's the way she is. That's why she's on this assignment.

FIONA. I don't mind saying I wish I were back with Louisa May Alcott. She never treated me this way.

PETER. You knew Louisa May Alcott?

FIONA. We never met, of course, but I was in her head. She gave me some pleasant things to say and a few laughs. I had a warm side. Lately, I'm all shriveled up into a typical spinster. Sometime, perhaps, they will call me down for a friendly mother.

KAY. *(egging her on)* Married or unmarried?

FIONA. *(rises)* It's no use talking to you. *(crosses to chair L.)* I shall sit over here with my knitting and think good thoughts. If I can.

PETER. *(rises)* I do apoligize if I've brought you down here for nothing.

FIONA. I suppose it isn't your fault entirely. You have to have the character lady in these stories and she's always the same.

KAY. *(crosses to her suitcase by the stairs)* I think I'll go upstairs and unpack.

FIONA. You're lucky if Addie hasn't beaten you to it.

KAY. I can handle her. I'll try a little kindness.

FIONA. That's a dig at me, I suppose. *(She has opened her knitting and brings out a partly completed piece of work. It is a horrendous mix of colors and has no definite shape and many partly completed armholes.)* Oh, no! Look at this. What is it? Is this your idea of a joke, young man?

PETER. *(goes to her)* I had nothing to do with that.

FIONA. Someone wasn't thinking nice thoughts when this was put into my bag. Knit. I always have to knit. *(looks at garment)* I suppose this is a sweater for an octopus.

KAY. You can always dye it grey when it's finished.

FIONA. *(starts knitting)* I'll be murdered long before that.

KAY. Perhaps not. We're free now and -

FIONA. Free or not, we're here to be murdered and we will be murdered. Mark my words.

PETER. I hadn't really planned the murders.

FIONA. You brought us here and murder was in your mind. So murder it will be.

PETER. *(to KAY)* Is that what must happen?

KAY. I'm not sure. Now that we're free, perhaps we can change things. Don't worry about it, Peter. We'll just pretend each moment as it comes. *(goes upstairs)* I'll try to soothe Addie down. *(from landing)* Oh, dear. She must be pregnant. She always is. *(exits)*

PETER. *(At a loss for a moment, he finally goes to FIONA.)* Miss Babcock - may I call you Fiona?

FIONA. You can do what you like. You're not trapped into a character like we are.

PETER. Fiona, I -

FIONA. Where did you ever dream up that name? It's preposterous. Fiona. Sounds like a rare tropical disease.

PETER. If I ever get back to writing again, I can change it.

FIONA. *(starting to melt towards him)* Would you? Would you really?

PETER. *(sits in chair down L)* What name would you like?

FIONA. Well, you won't laugh if I tell you?

PETER. No. Cross my heart and hope to - well, cross my heart.

FIONA. I always wanted to be named Glinda.

PETER. Glinda?

FIONA. I worked on THE WIZARD OF OZ.

PETER. You weren't -

FIONA. I was the Wicked Witch of the West for awhile but I got scratched with the rewrites. I wasn't mean enough.

PETER. You mean when I rewrite, if I make a big enough character change, another of you comes down and takes over?

FIONA. Precisely.

PETER. It's like an actor being replaced out of town.

FIONA. It's very humiliating going back up there knowing you've failed.

PETER. But it's not your fault. Sometimes we authors realize we've made a character too much one way or another and so we change it. You can't be blamed for that.

FIONA. That's a very nice thing to say. You're not as ter-

rible as I thought you were. Do you suppose I might have
a cup of tea?

PETER. *(pulls bell rope)* What's mine is yours.

FIONA. I think I'm mellowing a bit. Do you suppose it's
because I'm free?

PETER. Perhaps. *(goes to sofa L)* How free are you exactly? I mean, can you just leave here if you want and go
some place else?

FIONA. *(worried)* Oh, I don't think so. What would I use
for money? Of course, you might have made me an
heiress and I'll find huge wads of it in my suitcase. No,
Addie would have found it and stolen it. Besides, this is
where the mystery is set so I'd better stay here.

PETER. What happens to you if I leave?

FIONA. You can't go anywhere.

PETER. Sure I can.

FIONA. The phone is dead and the doors and windows
won't work for you. No, dear boy, you are trapped here
with the rest of us until we solve the mystery.

PETER. But there isn't any mystery.

FIONA. There will be. That's why you called us down,
isn't it?

PETER. Yes, but I didn't expect you to come.

FIONA. Then you shouldn't have invited us.

PETER. I didn't know you existed.

FIONA. Then you shouldn't be so rash with your
thoughts.

PETER. When I think of what I could have thought
of.

FIONA. Now you're sounding like Harold Pinter. I get
so confused working for him, I get a migraine and I'm out

of commission for weeks.

COGBURN. *(enters from dining room and goes to between chair and sofa)* You rang, sir?

FIONA. *(rises and points at him)* He did it!

COGBURN. Did what, Madame?

FIONA. *(goes to PETER)* Whatever was done. The butler did it.

PETER. Nothing's happened.

FIONA. *(goes to bench)* When it does, he did it.

COGBURN. *(to PETER)* Did you have to have that same character lady, sir? There are lots of others to choose from.

PETER. I rather like Fiona Babcock.

COGBURN. Fiona? *(tries to suppress a laugh)* Oh, sir.

FIONA. And what's so amusing?

COGBURN. You've had it this time, old girl. Fiona? You'll be the first one to get it.

PETER. You two must know each other.

FIONA. We have worked together at times. But butlers are getting so passé. *(goes above sofa)* Not much call for your type any more, is there?

COGBURN. I do very well in those historical biographies on Public Television.

PETER. Cogburn, Miss Babcock would enjoy a cup of tea. Would you mind?

COGBURN. Whether I mind or not is of no consequence, sir. It is my duty. Regardless of what I may think of her, I shall fetch her the most delicious tea it is possible to brew. *(exits)*

PETER. That really was very kind of him, now, wasn't it?

FIONA. *(to L of sofa)* He has no choice. He is a

butler. He has to butle. We can't throw off our traces all at once like a strip-teaser peeling off her garments. *(a sudden thought)* You don't have one of those here, do you?

PETER. Is it too late to think one up?

FIONA. *(sits in her chair and resumes knitting)* Much. We have to abide by the rules.

PETER. But I don't know them.

FIONA. What you have wrought we must not put asunder.

(ADDIE appears at the top of the stairs. She is the maid and wears a complete maid's outfit. ADDIE is a very young girl who is pert and vulnerable but is almost constantly in a state of emotional stress. She has a handkerchief to her face and is crying audibly. She speaks with a cockney accent.)

PETER. Now you're paraphrasing. *(sees ADDIE, rises and cross R)* Oh, my God, its another.

ADDIE. *(goes to him)* I'm sorry, sir. I just can't stop me tears.

FIONA. Don't cry, girl. It's your fault and you've got to live with it.

ADDIE. Beggin' your pardon, sir. I'll pull meself together in no time.

PETER. You must be Addie.

ADDIE. Can't you tell by me uniform? Ain't I what you expected?

PETER. I'd thought of a maid, yes, so I guess you'll have to do.

ADDIE. You'll keep me on then? I'd hate to be sent back with the rewrites.

ETER. Of course I'll keep you, if you can change one thing.

ADDIE. I'll do anything to oblige, I will. *(moves very close to him, looking up into his eyes)* Anything at all.

FIONA. Careful, Mr. Knight, she uses sex with abandon.

ADDIE. That one's jealous, that's what she is. *(to PETER)* Now what can I do for you?

PETER. It's your accent.

ADDIE. What's wrong with it?

PETER. You sound so British.

ADDIE. This ain't the Cornish Coast? Or the outskirts of London?

PETER. It's Vermont, the United States of America.

ADDIE. *(drops cockney accent)* Oh, that's a relief. I thought I was one of those cockneys again.

FIONA. Didn't you read your instructions? I know you were late for the briefing and I can imagine why.

ADDIE. She's always picking on me. I do my job as well as I can. *(goes below sofa)* I haven't been at it as long as she has.

FIONA. Hmph!

ADDIE. She's been doin' this since they carved mysteries on stone tablets.

FIONA. Well, I like that.

ADDIE. I'm glad you do because it's true.

PETER. *(crosses to ADDIE)* Can't we have a little peace between you two? This is all very confusing for me and I need a little help to get through it.

FIONA. Yes, Addie, keep your problems to yourself. Mr Knight has enough on his mind. He'd just started this story when we showed up and surprised him.

ADDIE. No one's been killed yet?

PETER. No.

ADDIE. *(glances at FIONA)* I know who I hope the first one is.

FIONA. It is usually the immoral maid.

ADDIE. Us poor servants always get it early on. You have a cook here, I hope. I'm rotten in the kitchen.

PETER. I don't really know. I was trying to keep the cast down so I'd thought of having the cook's arrival delayed.

ADDIE. By what?

PETER. I hadn't decided.

(phone rings)

ADDIE. Shall I answer It?

PETER. No, I will. *(starts for phone, turns to FIONA)* You said the phone was dead.

FIONA. You can't call out but you can receive one.

(phone rings again)

PETER. I wish you'd brought me a list of rules. *(into phone)* Hello ... yes, it is ... yes ... No, that's all right, I was expecting it ... Now, would you mind telling me what - ... Hello ... hello .. *(turns to others)* That was an employment agency. The cook has ptomaine poisoning and won't be here. *(hangs up)*

FIONA. Ate her own cooking no doubt.

ADDIE. Then who's going to prepare the meals?

PETER. Do you suppose the butler cooks?

ADDIE. *(crosses in)* A butler? Is he young and handsome?

FIONA. He's just your type.

COGBURN. *(enters with tea cup on tray, serves FIONA)* Your
tea, Miss Babcock.

FIONA. Thank you, Cogburn.

ADDIE. *(to PETER)* Why didn't you make him young
and handsome?

PETER. It never occurred to me. I suppose all butlers
were young at one time.

COGBURN. The young ones always get sent back with
the rewrites. *(goes below sofa to ADDIE)* I presume you know
your duties. You were late to the briefing because -

ADDIE. We've already been through that.

COGBURN. Sorry, I hate repetition.

ADDIE. I've never been free before. I mean I was always
stuck with the story and had no leeway. Do I have to
obey you?

COGBURN. You're the maid, aren't you?

ADDIE. Yes, but -

COGBURN. No buts. You do what I tell you. *(crosses to
dining room)* Come along now and help me prepare something edible for the guests.

ADDIE. *(to PETER)* Do I have to?

PETER. Would you mind?

COGBURN. Come along! *(ADDIE goes to him)* You're not
pregnant again, are you?

ADDIE. *(starts crying again)* I always am. Every time I
work on a story I'm pregnant. Or that one -*(points to
FIONA)* throws me out and then I get killed or jump in the
river. I *(voice trails off as she exits)* Maybe this time it will
be different.

COGBURN. *(as he follows her off)* I sincerely hope not.

FIONA. What did I tell you? Wanton. That child is wanton and worthless.

PETER. I thought you were mellowing.

FIONA. Around the edges only, but certainly not towards her sort.

PETER. *(goes above sofa)* Maybe she'll quit. I'm not holding her here. As a matter of fact, I'm not holding any of you here.

FIONA. *(rises, putting the knitting aside and crosses to him)* Don't try to side-step the issue, Mr. Knight, You thought us up and just as we arrived there was a cosmic something-or-other and we materialized - oh, how I hate that word - anyway, we are here and we can't leave until it's over.

PETER. How can it be over when I didn't think up the ending? *(goes to fireplace)* I didn't even think up the middle, only the beginning with an odd set of characters.

FIONA. Odd we may be but we've worked for better authors than you. *(sits on sofa)* I'll have you know that I was Shakespeare's Nurse for Juliet. Think that one over.

PETER. You didn't do such a good job. She killed herself and now I think I know why.

FIONA. A great pity. A charming girl, the one who played Juliet. We still exchange Christmas cards.

PETER. *(crosses in to R of sofa)* You have a post office - up there?

FIONA. As I recall, we have everything.

PETER. So how is Juliet?

FIONA. I run into her now and then and she deplores the lack of writing today as I do. She keeps getting called down for those television series where she's mugged, raped, beaten senseless and then saved after a commercial for a detergent. *(sighs)* Ah, give me the days of Shakespeare with a simple poison or a knife. So civilized.

PETER. *(crosses below her to bench)* I would hardly call HAMLET civilized with all the characters bloodied up at the end.

FIONA. But in iambic pentameter?

PETER. *(sits on bench)* Anyway, Shakespeare is in public domain. He doesn't get royalties.

FIONA. Are royalties so important?

PETER. If you had to work for a living you'd know what I'm talking about.

FIONA. Fortunately my vocation provides room and board and, I might add, fringe benefits.

PETER. Like what?

FIONA. Hospitalization for one, although I don't recall ever being that ill. Dead, yes, but ill, no.

PETER. Then you're content in that big library in the sky?

FIONA. *(rises)* Why, Mr. Knight, are you applying for a position with us?

PETER. No, I don't think it's for me.

FIONA. *(crosses to chair and picks up knitting)* You're an interesting type. I'm sure you'd get a lot of calls.

PETER. I don't want to be some other author's character.

FIONA. It's pleasant work, not dangerous at all. Of course you're frequently killed and, if they steal your body, you have to stay around for your funeral. Those are gruesome things. I don't like them at all.

PETER. *(rises and crosses in)* How did you start in this work?

FIONA. Which came first, Mr. Knight, the chicken or the egg? Did authors put characters into their heads or were they there already? The riddle of the Sphinx. *(looks at knitting)* This is appalling, isn't it?

PETER. Perhaps on your next call you'll get imported wool and you can make an afghan.

FIONA. That would be nice, wouldn't it?

LYDIA. *(comes downstairs She has changed to a blue dress and is very upset.)* Peter, I'm very upset with you.

PETER. Everyone seems to be upset with me.

LYDIA. *(sees FIONA)* Well, look who's here. I didn't know you were on call for this.

FIONA. I'm here to bring some moral values to the situation.

LYDIA. But nothing immoral has happened.

FIONA. It will. It always does.

LYDIA. Aren't you being the horse behind the cart to coin a phrase?

PETER. You two must have worked together before.

LYDIA. Innumerable times. *(to FIONA)* I'm called Lydia this time.

PETER. This is Fiona Babcock.

LYDIA. Fiona? *(not successfully suppresses a laugh)*

FIONA. I don't see why everybody finds that so amusing.

LYDIA. Fiona Babcock! *(sits on L end of sofa)* You've come a cropper this time.

FIONA. A rose by any other name would still smell. *(realizes what she has said)* That didn't turn out quite right.

PETER. *(crosses to FIONA)* I hope you ladies will get along while you're here. I can't put up with any fighting. *(goes to fireplace)* Now that you're free, as you call it, there's no reason not to be friends.

FIONA. I am civil to everyone.

LYDIA. Oh, I don't mind her. There's one in every book.

FIONA. *(She gathers up her knitting and rises.)* If you don't mind, I think I'll go and knit elsewhere. *(goes up C)* There must be a den or library. There always is in these old places.

PETER. To your left.

FIONA. Thank you. I presume I shall be called by midnight. I won't inherit anything, of course, I never do.

LYDIA. What good would it do you? You're always the first or second to get murdered.

FIONA. I don't mind. The sooner I get back to Homer the better.

PETER. Homer?

LYDIA. She lives with Homer.

PETER. *(feigning shock)* Fiona Babcock!

FIONA. *(She starts off U L above stairs.)* I'll have you know Homer is a cat. *(turns back)* And he is neutered. *(exits)*

LYDIA. Poor lady. She's never forgiven me for being called down by Somerset Maugham to play Sadie Thompson when I made that man of the cloth commit suicide.

PETER. *(goes to sofa R)* Was that you?

LYDIA. One of the few times I played a woman who was poor.

PETER. You're rich this time.

LYDIA. And that is precisely why I came down here. *(rises and goes to PETER)* Do you know who is upstairs in my bedroom?

PETER. I suppose it must be Jordan Dillingham.

LYDIA. Exactly. *(crosses below desk)* I go in to change and I'm down to my slip and he comes out of the bathroom rubbing scalp lotion on his head.

PETER. *(goes to her)* That wasn't my idea.

LYDIA. And he announces we're married again. *(pats PETER'S cheek)* Now, Peter, darling, couldn't you have been more original? Every time Dilly and I get married it never works. He's an insufferable bore and I find someone more attractive and younger.

PETER. But he has loads of money.

LYDIA. That's why I'm constantly marrying him. 'Tis always thus. *(goes below chair L)* Why can't you authors get some
original ideas?

PETER. *(crosses D C)* There aren't any left.

LYDIA. Maybe he'll get murdered. *(goes to PETER)* That's it, isn't it? He's the first one killed. Oh, thank you, Peter. *(kisses his cheek)*

PETER. I'm not sure.

LYDIA. Maybe at this very moment. The electric heater dropped into the bathtub. That's what I did to him in THE POSTMAN ALWAYS RINGS TWICE.

PETER. You're way ahead of me. I hadn't decided who would get murdered first.

LYDIA. *(goes to fireplace)* Then none of us knows what will happen. It's most unusual but rather titillating, isn't it? *(has a sudden thought)* I hope it isn't me. *(sits in chair L)* I like.

being able to do things I want for a change and not being hemmed in by a tiny brain. Not you, darling, I'm sure you're an excellent writer.

PETER. I've always tried to be. *(crosses to fireplace)* But why should anyone get murdered? I hadn't planned it out.

LYDIA. You are really very naive. All of us here, and whoever else you invited, are all specialists in murder. Naturally, there will be a lot of killings and lights going out and screams in the dark. You didn't start to write REBECCA OF SUNNYBROOK FARM, did you?

PETER. I was trying to write a fictional murder based on Norman Napier's death.

LYDIA. *(shivers)* Sadist, that's what Norman was.

PETER. You worked for him?

LYDIA. In St. Moritz. He would ski half the day and write half the night. In AVALANCHE OF MURDER he had me -

PETER. Buried under the snow -

LYDIA. With a ski pole through my heart.

PETER. That was a good mystery.

LYDIA. Good or bad, it was damned cold. And they didn't find me for three days. And to top it all, he dressed me in green. *(rises and turns for PETER'S inspection)* Don't I look better in blue, Peter? Tell me the truth.

PETER. *(rises and goes to her)* You look magnificent in blue.

LYDIA. I know. Kay won't wear blue, will she?

PETER. She might.

LYDIA. *(goes to foot of stairs)* I caught a glimpse of her in the hall upstairs. I suppose you had to have an ingenue?

PETER. It's usual.

LYDIA. *(comes down to above sofa)* Couldn't you have thought up someone not quite so nice? I always have to hate her when we work together and it's difficult because she's such a sweet little thing. But she's so young. She's always so damned young. *(slaps table for emphasis)*

PETER. *(crosses below sofa to L)* She is nice, isn't she?

LYDIA. *(circles to R)* There, you see. Right away you like her. Perhaps she'll be killed off first. That would be a plot twist, wouldn't it?

PETER. It's been done before.

LYDIA. Really?

PETER. *(sits on L end of sofa)* In LAURA. She was killed at the beginning.

LYDIA. *(sits R side of sofa)* But they only thought so and she appeared anyway. I mean really killed dead permanently. Then I'd have the men to myself.

PETER. Who would want to murder Kay?

LYDIA. *(laughs)* Silly boy.

(doorbell rings)

PETER. Now who is that?

LYDIA. Don't you know?

PETER. *(goes to U C looking off R)* I have no idea.

LYDIA. It's the unexpected guest. You must have one of those, a mysterious stranger who comes in out of the night?

PETER. I don't remember thinking about one.

COGBURN. *(comes in from dining room and crosses to PETER)* Excuse me, sir, but I have to let the unexpected guest in.

PETER. You think that's who it is, too?

COGBURN. *(crosses below PETER)* Naturally, sir. *(turns back)* It would be most unexpected if there were no unexpected guest. *(exits)*

PETER. *(goes to fireplace)* Why do you all know so much more than I do?

LYDIA. We've been doing this longer than you have.

PETER. Then tell me how it ends.

LYDIA. We only know each moment as it happens.

(DICK STANTON bursts in from up R. He is the juvenile and is very hearty, eager, and overly-pleasant. He is virile and shakes hands with authority making him something of a bull in a china shop. He wears a raincoat under which are grey flannels and a blazer. He carries a suitcase.)

DICK. *(puts suitcase down)* Sorry if I'm late. It isn't midnight, is it?

LYDIA. No, darling. You still have time.

DICK. Good. *(takes his coat off)* Beastly night out, isn't it? But then it always is when there's a will to be read.

COGBURN. May I, sir?

DICK. *(hands coat to COGBURN who takes it)* Oh, thanks - Cogburn, is it?

COGBURN. That's right, sir. *(exits off R)*

DICK. *(goes to sofa L)* They told me he would be called Cogburn this time. *(advances on PETER with his hand extended)* How do you do. You must be the unexpected guest.

PETER. Isn't that who you are?

DICK. No, I'm expected. I'm Dick Stanton.

LYDIA. You must have forgotten you had a juvenile.

PETER. I'm lucky I can remember who I am. How do you do.

DICK. *(They shake hands.)* And you are -?

LYDIA. Dick, this is our author.

DICK. Gee whiz, you're Peter Knight?

PETER. That's right.

DICK. *(slaps PETER on the shoulder)* It's great working for you. Never done it before.

(COGBURN crosses from U R to exit into the dining room.)

PETER. Thank you.

DICK. And to be free, too. That's the greatest. I'm not sure how to act.

LYDIA. You could try being a little less hearty.

DICK. Can't be any other way it seems. *(crosses to LYDIA)* Never worked with you before, either, but I've seen you around. Say, you look great in blue.

LYDIA. *(smiles)* Thank you. I'm Lydia.

DICK. That's a great name, too. *(crosses to sofa R looking over the room)* And look at this room. It's great.

PETER. That's great.

DICK. *(crosses to bookshelves behind desk as he cases the room)* I love working in gloomy old places. Never done one in Vermont before. In Maine once on the coast. *(turns to them)* Say, why do they always have these old places on the coast?

PETER. So someone can be pushed off a cliff.

LYDIA. And authors can have all that description about waves breaking on the rocks and surf rolling over a body.

DICK. *(looks at typewriter)* This place has enough atmosphere for FRANKENSTEIN.

LYDIA. Let's not get into monsters, please. They give me gooseflesh.

DICK. I don't mind them. *(to PETER as goes below typewriter to L of desk)* You might have seen some of my work. I was the lead in I WAS A TEENAGE WEREWOLF.

PETER. I somehow missed that one.

DICK. Say, where's the ingenue? They told me she was named Kay. Great name all right.

PETER. She's upstairs unpacking. *(DICK goes to foot of stairs.)* Maybe you won't like her.

DICK. No way. I have to like her. It's built into me.

LYDIA. And she has to like him.

DICK. *(crosses down to desk)* You're darn right she does.

KAY. *(appears at top of stairs)* Dick! Dick Stanton! *(She rushes down and into his arms. They kiss.)*

DICK. Kay, it's you. Sorry I'm late.

KAY. I hoped you'd get here. The storm is terrible.

DICK. I was afraid the bridge would be washed out.

LYDIA. *(to PETER)* A washed out bridge wouldn't have stopped him.

DICK. I'd have swum across to get to you.

KAY. I'm so glad you're here. *(her head on his chest)* I'm so frightened.

PETER. Of what?

KAY. *(head comes up and she looks at him)* I don't know really. I always say that.

PETER. There is nothing to be frightened about.

LYDIA. I bet there is. We'll find out at midnight.

DICK. *(His arm around KAY, he pulls her to him.)* Aren't you going to leave us alone? It's customary for us to have a love scene.

LYDIA. *(rises, links her arm through PETER'S and takes him U C)* Come on. Peter, let's let them have their moment alone. It's a lot of foolishness and doesn't change the plot at all. We'll needle Miss Babcock in the library.

PETER. I don't want to go.

LYDIA. This is the way it has to be. *(as LYDIA pulls him out to library)*

PETER. We won't be long.

LYDIA. If my husband gets killed, then maybe we could have a mature love scene.

DICK. *(starts to kiss KAY)* I'm so glad to see you.

KAY. *(breaks away below sofa)* You don't have to do that, Dick. We're alone now.

DICK. *(goes to her)* Can you think of a better time?

KAY. But we're free. We don't have to be in love.

DICK. I know we're free but I still love you. I think.

KAY. You're just used to it, that's all. You always love the damsel in distress.

DICK. And she always loves me.

KAY. And I do. I suppose I do. I always have.

DICK. Of course you do. Besides, if I wasn't here who would save you at the end?

KAY. *(goes to fireplace)* Maybe I won't need saving this time.

DICK. That's a stupid thing to say. *(goes to her and puts his arms around her from behind)* You always need saving at the last moment and not a second sooner.

KAY. *(turns to him)* I wish one of you would show up early and not just ten seconds before the bomb goes off.

DICK. I'm just not capable of getting there any quicker.

KAY. It makes me very nervous.

DICK. Come on, let's have our nice little love scene now. *(tries to kiss her)*

KAY. *(breaks away R)* No. Let's wait until later, until after the will is read.

DICK. I have never been turned down by the ingenue yet.

KAY. *(goes to bench, her back to him)* I'm not turning you down. I'm postponing you.

DICK. All right, have it your way. *(picks up his suitcase)* I'll go and unpack. Where do I go?

KAY. *(goes to him)* Upstairs. You must be the second on the right. It's very masculine looking.

DICK. Boy, I can't wait for the will to be read. That's always the most exciting part. *(on landing)*

KAY. Not if you're the ingenue. That's when they set me up to be killed.

DICK. But I'll save you. And I'll try to be early this time. *(looks down the hallway upstairs)* Boy, look at the gloomy hallway. This is great. *(exits)*

KAY. *(moves to table above sofa, looks around and suddenly realizes she is alone)* Oh, I'm alone. I shouldn't be left alone. The ingenue never should be left alone. There's a secret panel and a gloved hand will come out or a hooded figure bent on my destruction. *(crosses U C and calls towards library)* Peter! Peter!

PETER. *(off stage)* I'm here.

KAY. *(moves down into room)* Come quickly, please.

PETER. *(rushes in)* Kay, what is it?

KAY. *(into his arms)* Oh, Peter, I'm so glad you're here.

I'm so frightened.

PETER. That's exactly what you said to your boy friend.

KAY. It is, isn't it? *(crosses to bench)*

PETER. Word for word.

KAY. And now I've said it to you. That must mean something.

PETER. I think it does. *(goes to her)* Now what are you frightened of?

KAY. I don't know. I was alone and I should never be left alone. It's always dangerous. Authors think up reasons for everyone leaving me alone and then something horrifying happens.

PETER. It's all right. I'm here now.

KAY. Yes, you're here. *(They kiss.)*

PETER. That wasn't at all unreal.

KAY. *(breaks away L)* I shouldn't do that. I'm in love with Dick Stanton. That's the way it's written.

PETER. *(goes to her)* But you're free now. You can do what you want.

KAY. People always fall in love so quickly in stories but it isn't that way in real life, is it?

PETER. It's never been that way with me.

KAY. *(crosses below him to his R)* You're in love with someone then?

PETER. I was once, but no more. She married a man who went into microchips before anyone knew what they were.

KAY. Was that good?

PETER. For him, for her, but not for me. Now she's living happily in a penthouse overlooking the East River.

KAY. Poor Peter.

PETER. It's surprising how quickly I've recovered.

KAY. *(sits sofa R)* I'm glad.

PETER. *(sits next to her)* I wish we'd met somewhere else but here in the middle of this.

KAY. So do I.

PETER. We could go out on a date, catch a movie, and -

KAY. Go to a little restaurant you know. Chianti and red-checkered tablecloths. It would become "our place".

PETER. Just what I was going to say.

KAY. Authors always have an "our place" like that in their stories.

PETER. But I mean it for real. There's a McDonalds down route seven that doesn't have candles, but it has -

KAY. *(laughs)* Oh, Peter, it sounds heavenly.

PETER. Afterwards we could come back here and sit in front of the fire.

KAY. *(her fingers on his lips)* No, Peter, don't go on.

PETER. Why not?

KAY. I'm not the girl for you. I'm not real.

PETER. But you're here.

KAY. For the moment. *(rises and crosses U R)* I'm like - what was that Scottish story I was in about the town?

PETER. BRIGADOON?

KAY. Yes. It comes to life once every hundred years for a day. But I never come to life, Peter, not really to your kind of life. Oh, an evening like this maybe, now and then, but I'm still never a really, truly live person. I'm always tied to my character.

PETER. *(goes to her)* Couldn't I rethink you and bring you back?

KAY. They might send someone else of my type and anyway, there probably wouldn't be any lightning and cosmic thing-a-ma-jig and we wouldn't even be visible to you.

PETER. Then we'll never have that date?

KAY. No, Peter, never. Promise you won't go running about the moors calling for me like Heathcliffe did for Cathy.

PETER. There aren't any moors in Vermont, just fields and they're covered with either cows or condominiums.

KAY. *(laughs)* You are nice, Peter.

COGBURN. *(enters from dining room)* Pardon me, sir, but it is approaching the witching hour.

PETER. It can't be midnight already.

COGBURN. A few minutes before to be precise.

PETER. But it's only late afternoon.

KAY. *(sits on bench)* Time is different for you now, Peter. You must know that. You authors just write "three hours later" or "after dinner that evening" and it is just that. So if Cogburn says it is almost midnight then it is almost midnight.

PETER. We authors do play havoc with time, don't we?

COGBURN. Might I suggest we gather the guests in here for the reading of the will?

PETER. If it must be.

COGBURN. *(goes to foot of stairs)* It must be.

KAY. For once, I hope everything isn't left to me in some peculiar codocil.

COGBURN. Begging your pardon, sir.

PETER. Yes Cogburn.

COGBURN. There is something I have had a great desire to do for ages and now that I am free and my character restraints are loosening, may I have your permission to do it?

PETER. Enjoy yourself, Cogburn.

COGBURN. Thank you, sir. *(At foot of stairs, he suddenly screams out.)* Reading of the will down here! Let's get a move on!

KAY. *(shocked, but she still giggles)* Why, Cogburn.

PETER. Good Lord!

COGBURN. *(resumes his former dignity)* I found that most refreshing.

PETER. I'm glad someone is happy.

COGBURN. *(crosses to above sofa)* Might I suggest I serve the guests a libation?

PETER. Brandy would be appropriate if we have any.

COGBURN. I shall ascertain. Excuse me, sir. *(exits dining room)*

KAY. Who would have thought he had that raucous behavior in him?

PETER. It makes me wonder what other hidden emotions are repressed in the others.

FIONA. *(comes in from library with her knitting)* May I ask what that call to arms was?

PETER. Just Cogburn requesting everyone's pleasure in here.

FIONA. *(goes to below chair L)* I've never heard anything so crass in my life. I dropped two stitches.

KAY. He was just letting down his hair.

FIONA. Is there no decorum left in the world? I appeal to you, Mr. Knight, to keep your characters under control.

PETER. I've lost control. You're free now.

FIONA. *(sits and resumes knitting)* But certainly not free to behave that much out of character. It's deplorable.

LYDIA. *(comes in from library)* What has Cogburn been drinking?

FIONA. He's letting down his hair, what there is of it.

LYDIA. *(goes to fireplace)* We're in Vermont. Suppose a

herd of hogs answers his call and comes galloping in here?

FIONA. I don't believe hogs gallop.

LYDIA. *(sits in chair D L)* You have no sense of humor.

FIONA. And you have no sense of manners.

DICK. *(comes downstairs)* I must say, that was an announcement. I didn't think Cogburn had it in him.

PETER. We're all rather surprised.

(JORDAN DILLINGHAM appears on the landing. He is in his sixties, well-dressed and groomed. JORDAN is successful and looks it but one feels it is not entirely through legitimate means that he has reached his position.)

JORDAN. I trust someone has given that butler his notice. I think dignity should prevail on these occasions. Good evening, everyone. I am Jordan Dillingham, the lawyer. *(He comes down the stairs and goes to sofa L.)* Mr. Stanton, nice to see you again.

DICK. *(rises as they shake hands)* It's great seeing you, sir.

JORDAN. *(crosses below DICK to KAY)* Ah, Kay. I've been looking forward to working with you again. *(has hold of her hand and doesn't let it go)*

KAY. I don't see why. Every time you read a will I get plunged into mortal danger. *(tries to remove her hand from his)*

LYDIA. Dilly! Let go of the child's hand. You're old enough to be her grandfather.

JORDAN. *(Drops her hand and goes to LYDIA. DICK sits on sofa.)* And my charming wife. We make such an attractive couple, don't you think? She's as beautiful as my money and three face-lifts can make her.

LYDIA. Don't pay any attention to him. Senility is running rampant through every one of his varicose veins.

JORDAN. Once Lydia decides to step into old age gracefully, we'll retire to St. Petersburg and play shuffleboard. *(to FIONA)* And Miss Babcock. Charmed.

FIONA. Good evening, Mr. Dillingham.

JORDAN. I must say what your knitting lacks in skill it makes up for in originality.

FIONA. I didn't start this. It was this way when I got here.

JORDAN. I wasn't told your first name this time. Agatha again? Or Martha? Perhaps even Matilda?

FIONA. Never mind.

LYDIA. It's Fiona.

JORDAN. Fiona? *(enjoys himself with a laugh)* Well, I must say it fits you like a glove. *(turns to PETER)* Ah, you must be the unexpected guest.

PETER. No, I'm Peter Knight.

LYDIA. He's our author.

JORDAN. So you're the one responsible for all this.

PETER. Only part of it. I started it and -

JORDAN. And we have to finish it. *(crosses to R of desk)* Shall we proceed. I have the will right here. *(takes it from his pocket)*

FIONA. It isn't midnight yet.

JORDAN. You're right, Fiona. We must wait for the clock to strike.

COGBURN. *(Enters from dining room with ADDIE behind him. She holds a tray of assorted containers ranging from a bud vase to jelly glasses, etc., six in all. They contain brandy to about one-quarter full.)* Beg pardon, sir, but there is a slight disaster which I have tried to overcome.

PETER. *(goes above sofa)* Yes, Cogburn.

COGBURN. There doesn't seem to be an ample supply of cordial glasses or brandy snifters.

ADDIE. *(fighting back her usual tears)* I hate to pass these around. I'm so embarrassed.

COGBURN. Had I known, I, of course, would have brought some with me. I did my best with what containers I could find.

PETER. If you've done your best, Cogburn, we can't ask for more.

COGBURN. I did find an unopened bottle of superior cognac. May we serve?

PETER. Please do. *(crosses to bench and sits)*

FIONA. *(She shakes her head as ADDIE passes tray. COGBURN goes between sofa and chair.)* I am of the opinion we should refrain from drinking. We must keep a clear head for what is bound to occur this evening.

LYDIA. I'm of the opinion we should all drink as much and as quickly as possible.

JORDAN. *(as ADDIE serves LYDIA)* My wife will drink anything. You should taste her Lestoil martini.

LYDIA. *(as ADDIE goes to DICK)* Go ahead, ridicule me in public. It's your favorite sport. I warn you, one day you'll say too much and I'll -

JORDAN. And you'll what?

LYDIA. Never mind. *(DICK has taken drink. KAY refuses.)*

JORDAN. A clue, Mr. Author. Note that my wife hates me enough to make a threatening statement. You must sprinkle these incidents around to confuse the reader.

KAY. Please. Can't we read the will without all this bickering?

PETER. *(to ADDIE as he takes the bud vase)* Thank you. Cogburn, you're right. This is a most unusual glass.

(ADDIE crosses above desk and down to JORDAN who takes a glass, then she joins COGBURN.)

COGBURN. I believe it is a bud vase, sir.

LYDIA. It's what's in it that counts.

FIONA. *(to ADDIE)* Will you stop that sniveling, girl.

ADDIE. I'm sorry.

JORDAN. The poor maid being picked on again, is she? *(to ADDIE)* Undoubtedly you're pregnant.

ADDIE. *(weeping)* I always am.

JORDAN. As long as your tears didn't water the drinks. Now, are we all ready for the reading?

PETER. No. I don't even know who's will it is.

JORDAN. Parker Humberton, of course.

PETER. I had so many people in mind but I hadn't decided which one to choose. Who is - was - Parker Humberton?

JORDAN. A very rich and -

LYDIA. - eccentric recluse. You must know that.

JORDAN. My wife is correct for once. Parker Humberton was an inventor who struck it rich.

PETER. How?

JORDAN. I believe he invented the paper clip. As a child, he worked the farm on this very land. At night, instead of drinking with the other youths and chasing the farmers' daughters. Parker would sit home and read Edgar Allen Poe by a kerosene lamp. After he made his fortune, he had this house built as he believed Mr. Poe would have wanted it.

LYDIA. Is that eccentric enough for you, Peter?

PETER. I couldn't have thought that up.

KAY. But he was a kind and lovable man, wasn't he, Mr. Dillingham?

JORDAN. Naturally you would think so.

KAY. I always have a soft spot for elderly eccentrics.

JORDAN. All of you have been called here for the reading as all of you are in the will. *(COGBURN and ADDIE start to leave.)* Including the servants.

COGBURN. Me, sir?

ADDIE. And me?

JORDAN. That is correct.

COGBURN. But I only served Mr. Humberton with unfailing loyalty for thirty-five years. I didn't expect any small token.

LYDIA. But a large one, I bet.

ADDIE. *(moves above sofa)* And me? Why me? I only worked here for the past six months.

FIONA. I'd assume, due to your condition. Mr. Humberton was not quite as old and feeble as we have been led to believe.

ADDIE. *(puts tray on table)* That's a disgusting thing to say. It might be true but it's still disgusting. *(goes to COGBURN)*

JORDAN. Miss Babcock - Fiona - *(He loves saying the word.)* You are mentioned because you and Mr. Humberton were pen pals.

FIONA. I understand that. Please continue.

JORDAN. *(obviously enjoying this)* You had corresponded with him for the past five years and, I believe, sent him your photograph.

FIONA. Yes, yes, go on to the others.

JORDAN. And, I believe, the photograph you sent was not actually one of yourself.

FIONA. That's irrelevant.

JORDAN. You sent him a centerfold from - Playboy, wasn't it?

LYDIA. Fiona!

ADDIE. Oh, Miss Babcock, I am shocked.

DICK. That magazine has good articles in it.

KAY. Is it like the National Geographic?

FIONA. I was merely giving the old man something to live for. It was a charitable act.

(ADDIE cries again.)

LYDIA. Addie believes charity begins at home, don't you, dear?

JORDAN. To continue. Kay is here as the only surviving relative. She is Mr. Humberton's niece's adopted daughter, but first Mr. Humberton brought her here from the orphanage.

KAY. Then I was legally adopted by his niece.

DICK. She must have been a great mother to you.

KAY. She was such a kind lady.

JORDAN. And Dick Stanton, your father was a worker for Mr. Humberton and helped him invent the paper clip.

DICK. But one of the paper clips fell into his peanut butter sandwich at lunch one day.

KAY. Oh, Dick how horrible.

DICK. He choked so much he passed out. It affected his brain and he had to quit and did menial labor at a fertilizer plant.

JORDAN. And I, of course, was Mr. Humberton's solicitor and devoted my life to helping the deceased.

LYDIA. And helping yourself to his money, I imagine.

JORDAN. If I did, then you reaped the benefits.

LYDIA. I worked for it. I doted on the old fool. I addressed his Christmas cards, represented him at charity functions, and saved him from going out into the world.

JORDAN. I think that takes care of everyone.

PETER. Except me.

JORDAN. Ah, the unexpected guest.

DICK. And the author.

JORDAN. I don't quite understand what you are doing here but you can't very well leave since you began this.

PETER. I didn't know what I was getting into. *(clock starts striking twelve)*

JORDAN. Midnight! I shall now open the will. *(tears seal on the envelope)*

KAY. I'm so frightened.

DICK. Of what?

KAY. Of this evening. I know it will be dangerous for me.

JORDAN. *(reads)* "I, Parker Humberton, being of sound mind and body -."

FIONA. Which is questionable.

ADDIE. His body was sound all right.

FIONA. You should know.

JORDAN. "etc. etc. etc." Ah, here we are - "do hereby leave my entire estate in bearer bonds."

LYDIA. No cash?

JORDAN. Bearer bonds are as good as cash.

LYDIA. Thank God for that.

JORDAN. "In bearer bonds except for petty cash which is to be distributed among those present."

LYDIA. Petty cash? How much does that mean?

JORDAN. A few hundred dollars.

DICK. That's great.

FIONA. But who gets the bonds?

JORDAN. The bonds I hereby will to - *(looks from one to the other)*

FIONA. Go on, don't stop there.

KAY. I hope it's not me.

JORDAN. "- to Kay Kelsey".

KAY. *(rises)* It is me.

DICK. *(rises)* Congratulations.

LYDIA. The senile idiot.

JORDAN. There's more. *(DICK and KAY resume their seats as he reads.)* "Since I do not trust my solicitor and friend, Jordan Dillingham -".

LYDIA. Would you read that again, please.

JORDAN. Poor Humberton. He must have been really round the bend when he wrote this. "... solicitor and friend, to turn over these bonds so I have hidden them in a safe place for Kay."

KAY. Where could he have hidden them?

JORDAN. "If she remembers that happy Christmas she spent here when she was three years old, then she will know where the bonds are."

KAY. It was such a happy Christmas.

JORDAN. "If that Christmas didn't mean as much to her as it did to me, then she doesn't deserve them and they will decay into useless dust."

KAY. *(rises and goes to sofa R)* No, no, I don't want them. Please, someone else take them.

LYDIA. I will, gladly.

JORDAN. There we are. The will is read and now the stage is set for murder. *(a bright flash of lightning and the lights go to black)*

PETER. *(as there is a general ad-lib)* Don't anyone move. I'll get the flashlight.

JORDAN. At least we can still drink.

LYDIA. I should have known this would happen.

FIONA. It always does.

DICK. *(after a scream is heard from KAY)* Kay, Kay, are you all right?

KAY. Something - something brushed against me.

COGBURN. Can I help you, sir?

PETER. No, here it is. *(Flashlight from desk drawer goes on. He shines it to where KAY was.)* Kay, where are you?

DICK. She was right here.

PETER. Kay.

KAY. *(rises from behind sofa)* I'm all right, Peter. I ducked down here.

PETER. Everyone else OK ?*(light to LYDIA)*

LYDIA. I'm still here.

FIONA. *(as he shines light on her)* No one killed me yet.

COGBURN. *(when light reaches them)* ADDIE and I are still here, sir.

ADDIE. I'm so scared.

FIONA. Show some pluck, girl. No one would want to kill you.

PETER. And Mr. Dillingham. *(light to him / He is slumped forward in his chair.)*

LYDIA. Dilly!

DICK. *(rises)* Good Lord!

KAY. Oh, no. Is he - is he -?

PETER. Yes, he's dead.

KAY. Oh, no!

FIONA. But how? We didn't hear anything.

PETER. *(takes bud vase from JORDAN'S hand and smells it)* It smells of bitter almonds.

FIONA. Cyanide!

KAY. But Peter, that glass -

LYDIA. It's the bud vase.

KAY. That glass was yours, Peter. He must have picked it up in the dark by mistake.

PETER. Then whoever put the cyanide in it thought I would drink it.

LYDIA. Precisely. *(She has a faint smile on her lips.   rises)*

FIONA. *(smiles / rises)* This is a murder mystery, isn't it?

PETER. Then one of you -?

COGBURN. Yes, sir, one of us.

ADDIE. It must be one of us.

PETER. But I created you.

KAY. Yes, you did.

DICK. And one of us wants you dead. *(rises)*

PETER. But which one of you? Which?

(He shines the light from one to the other. They look back at him impassively as

THE CURTAIN FALLS

ACT TWO

Out Of Sight ... Out Of Murder
by
Fred Carmichael

SCENE 1: *(A short time later. ADDIE is looking up the stairs, KAY is seated on the R side of the sofa, LYDIA is standing in front of the fireplace, FIONA is in her chair, and PETER is standing above the bench. Pause. LYDIA goes to drink her brandy, then stops and looks at it.)*

LYDIA. I suppose I'd better not drink this.

PETER. Does it smell of bitter almonds?

LYDIA. *(sniffs it)* Just cognac.

PETER. Since you've already drunk some, you might as well finish it.

FIONA. You believe that just one of the drinks was poisoned? Yours?

PETER. *(moves to R of sofa)* It appears that way.

KAY. *(goes to PETER)* You didn't sip any before the will was read?

PETER. Not that I remember.

KAY. Then the poison could have been in there when it was served?

ADDIE. *(by sofa L)* Don't look at me. It was Cogburn who poured the drinks in the pantry. I just helped. *(crosses back to dining room arch)*

PETER. The cyanide could have been put in when the lights went out.

LYDIA. Someone brushed by Kay in the dark. It must have been the killer.

ADDIE. But why would anyone want to kill poor Mr. Dillingham?

LYDIA. *(laughs as she crosses to sofa and sits)* Silly girl. I can give you a thousand reasons. He has cheated people all his life. Remember the big Compton Computer fraud? Everyone knew he was guilty of that but he escaped through a legal loophole. He invested Humberton's money in it but the old boy outsmarted him, sold the stock and bought the bearer bonds. Thousands of investors lost their life's savings.

KAY. But wasn't it Peter the killer was after?

PETER. Not necessarily. In the dark, the murderer might have thought it was Dillingham's glass.

FIONA. It doesn't amount to a row of pins. I'm just as glad he was the first one murdered.

PETER. The first? You talk as if there will be more.

FIONA. *(knits as she looks up at him)* My dear Mr. Knight, you are an author. Did you ever know a murder story with only one murder?

PETER. Come to think of it -

FIONA. You didn't! Of course there will be another murder. Perhaps more. It's quite fashionable to have everyone killed off these days. Except the culprit, of course.

KAY. *(crosses and sits on the down stage of the bench)* Someone will try to kill me next. I know it. *(DICK and COGBURN come down the stairs.)*

DICK. We got the body up there all right.

COGBURN. Mr. Dillingham looked so peaceful lying there in the East Room. We folded his hands across his chest. *(goes to dining room arch)*

LYDIA. That's the way he'd want it, protecting his wallet.

FIONA. He ought to know he can't take it with him.

DICK. *(moves to above sofa)* Are you all right, Kay?

KAY. Yes, Dick, but you must be exhausted.

DICK. He was a dead weight.

LYDIA. I find that in rather bad taste.

DICK. Sorry.

LYDIA. It just occurred to me.

PETER. What?

LYDIA. I'm a widow now. *(starts a rather fake cry)* My poor husband is dead and gone. Oh, Dilly, why did you leave me?

KAY. *(sits on sofa and comforts her)* There, there, Lydia. Time will ease your pain.

FIONA. What pain? She's as delighted as a dog with a new bone. You don't believe those tears, do you?

DICK. *(by sofa L)* I think they're great.

KAY. *(gently to LYDIA)* They don't sound very genuine, Lydia.

LYDIA. *(rises and goes to bench)* I'm doing the best I can. One has to cry when one's husband is murdered. I always do. It's one of the things I do best.

FIONA. What's the other? Murdering him?

LYDIA. Not this time, Fiona. *(to PETER as DICK sits by KAY)* I admit I have killed my husbands in other stories but not now. Why would I jeopardize my freedom? *(sits on bench)*

KAY. I believe you.

FIONA. You always believe everyone.

COGBURN. Excuse me, sir but there's nothing furthur you want of us right now, is there?

PETER. No, thank you, Cogburn.

COGBURN. Come along, Addie.

ADDIE. But what if you're the murderer? I don't want to be alone with you in the kitchen with all those knives. He even has an electric one.

COGBURN. If I'd wanted to kill you I'd have done it before this.

ADDIE. Maybe you're just waiting for the right moment.

COGBURN. *(as he guides her out the dining room)* Then you'll soon find out, won't you?

FIONA. As if anyone would waste a good murder on that one.

DICK. Shouldn't we call the police or something? They might send a good detective like Hercule Poirot or someone.

FIONA. Or Miss Marple. One of the few times a spinster was put to good use. But you can't borrow from Agatha Christie, can you?

PETER. I'm afraid not. This isn't the only time I wished I were A. Conan Doyle. *(sits by LYDIA on the bench)*

DICK. Then we have to discover who did it?

PETER. I guess so.

LYDIA. Let's get to the important thing.

KAY. You mean clues?

LYDIA. *(rises)* I mean bonds. "Pay to Bearer" bonds. *(goes to sofa)* There's a fortune here somewhere and you know where it is.

KAY. But I don't.

LYDIA. The will said you did.

KAY. Mr. Humberton said it was something to do with Christmas when I was three years old. I don't know what he meant.

DICK. I believe her.

LYDIA. *(moves above sofa)* Well, I don't.

KAY. I don't want them anyway.

FIONA. Oh, come now.

LYDIA. You ingenues always talk like that. There is no one who doesn't want more money.

KAY. I just want to find the murderer and see he is brought to justice.

LYDIA. *(moves down to R of sofa)* Or perhaps you want to murder all of us so we can't find the money. Once you have this place to yourself, you can take the place apart brick by brick.

PETER. *(rises)* Kay, do you know where the bonds are?

KAY. No, I tell you. No.

DICK. *(rises)* I believe you.

LYDIA. Will you stop saying that! *(She crosses above desk.)*

KAY. Wait. Now I remember. Mr. Humberton read to me that Christmas Eve. Here in front of the fire. That was the first time I remember hearing A CHRISTMAS CAROL.

LYDIA. Then the bonds are in the book. *(rushes to the bookshelves behind the desk)*

DICK. *(crosses below desk to bookshelves and pushes LYDIA upstage)* Get away from there. Those bonds are ours. We need them.

PETER. *(goes above desk)* What do you mean "ours"? They're Kay's.

DICK. *(goes below desk to KAY)* I meant ours when we're married.

KAY. *(rises)* Dick!

FIONA. I smell a rat.

PETER. You're engaged?

KAY. Not that I know of.

DICK. We will be. I'm going to propose tonight.

PETER. Are you going to accept?

KAY. I don't know. *(turns front)* This is so sudden.

FIONA. Can't you ever think of something different to say?

DICK. Of course you'll accept. Everyone knows we're going to get married.

PETER. Everyone it seems but Kay.

DICK. *(turns KAY to him)* You've got to marry me. That's the way it always is, the juvenile and the ingenue. We'll be happy. I know we will. We'll have all that money and - *(stops)*

KAY. Is it me you want or the bonds?

FIONA. Did he propose before you were an heiress?

KAY. No.

LYDIA. I think we have an ambitious, money-grubbing juvenile for a change. Good for you, Peter.

PETER. I didn't write this part, remember?

KAY. Dick, be honest with me.

DICK. All right then. Those bonds are rightfully mine. My mother invested her life savings in Compton Computer after Dad was killed at the fertilizer plant.

FIONA. Where?

DICK. *(to FIONA)* The fertilizer plant. He got caught in a machine and now he's spread out somewhere in Vermont.

KAY. *(sinks on sofa R)* How terrible.

DICK. Humberton had invested in Compton Computer with his profits from the paper clips. Part of those profits rightfully belonged to Dad. When Humberton turned the money into bearer bonds I figured that part of that still belonged to Dad.

KAY. If I find them, I shall give them to your mother.

DICK. But I think Mr. Dillingham thought the will would tell where the bonds were and he'd get hold of them.

LYDIA. That sounds like my husband.

PETER. *(goes to sofa R)* But there was Humberton's cryptic message about Christmas.

FIONA. And then Jordan was killed.

LYDIA. By you, Dick.

DICK. No, I didn't do it.

LYDIA. *(goes down to bench and sits)* You thought my husband would find another legal loophole to get the bonds. With him out of the way and with you marrying Kay, the bonds would be yours.

DICK. I'd get them by marrying Kay, yes, but I didn't kill Jordan.

FIONA. I, for one, am having a good time. We have a juvenile who is a cad.

DICK. I didn't kill him, I tell you.

KAY. I believe you, Dick. *(DICK sits next to her on the sofa.)*

FIONA. You're being taken in by him.

KAY. I can't marry you though.

DICK. But -

KAY. *(her fingers on his lips)* I would have, Dick. I have before in other stories and I'm sure I will again, but not this time.

DICK. There's someone else?

KAY. *(with a glance at PETER)* I can't say.

DICK. *(with a deadly look at PETER)* If there is, he'd better watch his step.

LYDIA. Up comes another threat or another red herring. Take your choice.

FIONA. Isn't anyone going to find that book with the bonds?

PETER. *(crosses to shelves)* I should assume a man as eccentric as Humberton would have his books alphabetized. *(looks through them)* D - D - D - Dickens. A TALE OF TWO CITIES. NICHOLAS NICKLEBY -

FIONA. I helped him write that. I was the woman who -

PETER. Here it is. A CHRISTMAS CAROL.

LYDIA. The pages have been cut out and the bonds are there.

PETER. *(opens the book)* It's just a book. No bonds.

DICK. So they're somewhere else.

PETER. You'll have to think, Kay. What else happened here that fateful Christmas?

KAY. I don't know. I was so young. I can't remember.

LYDIA. I don't know why people in these stories don't just leave the money in a nice lump sum in a desk drawer.

KAY. If I find them, you can have them, Dick?

DICK. You mean that?

KAY. Yes, I do.

FIONA. What a combination, young and stupid.

LYDIA. You're a fool, Kay.

KAY. Maybe I'll wish I hadn't given them up when I'm your age.

FIONA. Score one for the ingenue. *(She has been searching in her bag. She rises.)* I've been robbed.

PETER. What's missing?

FIONA. My peppermints. I know I had them in here.

LYDIA. I really can't concern myself with peppermints.

FIONA. I must have left them upstairs.

DICK. *(starts to rise)* Shall I get them for you?

FIONA. *(goes upstairs with knitting bag)* No, thank you. I don't want anyone wandering around my room.

LYDIA. This is an arbitrary exit if you ask me. I think Fiona's going to get murdered.

FIONA. *(on landing)* I doubt it. You're all down here and the servants are in the kitchen. Just see that you all stay here until I return. *(exits)*

(PETER sits in desk chair.)

LYDIA. I wouldn't be surprised if we never see her again.

DICK. I really do want to apologize, Kay. I may have taken advantage of you but underneath it all, I am very fond of you.

KAY. Thank you, Dick. And the bonds are yours if we find them. They're for your mother.

DICK. My mother's gravely ill, but now I can give her a decent burial. I want to have her ashes scattered over the fields of Vermont so she'll be with Dad.

KAY. What a nice thought.

LYDIA. Remind me not to eat anything grown in Vermont.

DICK. *(rises)* Say, I really do have to go upstairs. Do you think Fiona will scream bloody murder?

PETER. Can't you wait till she comes back?

DICK. No. You see - I have to - well, there isn't one downstairs and -

LYDIA. *(laughs)* The poor boy wants to powder his nose. *(rises and meets him at the foot of stairs)* Come along, Dickie Boy, I'll go with you and chaperone Fiona.

DICK. You two stay together. Don't go wandering off. *(exits)*

LYDIA. *(on landing)* I want to start packing Jordan's things. If I give them to the Salvation Army it's tax deductible. *(as she exits)* Dick, don't forget to jiggle the handle.

PETER. *(goes to KAY)* You're safe with me.

KAY. *(rises and goes into his arms)* I know. I'm so frightened.

PETER. Not of me?

KAY. Not of you, Peter, but of something. I'm always frightened until the story is over and I'm saved.

PETER. But no one's tried to harm you.

KAY. *(breaks away and goes to fireplace)* They will. If I find the bonds, they'll try to kill me to get them and if I don't, they'll kill all of us and really search for them.

PETER. *(crosses in L)* You're sure you don't remember anything about that Christmas?

KAY. I'm trying but I was only three.

PETER. You must have been a beautiful child.

KAY. Yes, I was. I'm always described that way. *(goes to him)* But what about you? Aren't you scared? Someone tried to murder you. Someone you invented got free and is turning on you.

PETER. *(crosses to bench)* It could be any of them. How would I know which one?

KAY. Perhaps it's something you were thinking in your subconscious. Do you remember even having a passing thought of who would be the murdered?

PETER. No. *(sits on up stage end of bench)* I'm like you. Neither of us remembers what we should.

KAY. *(sits beside him)* We are so alike, Peter. If only I didn't have to go back.

PETER. But you don't now that you're free.

KAY. This will end somehow, some time. And when it does, I'll go back to be some other author's ingenue but it will never be the same.

PETER. For me either.

KAY. *(faces front)* I'm lying. It will be the same. Emotions will fade away and I'll only remember the facts of the story, not the emotions.

PETER. *(turns her to him)* Then we have to make the most of this moment.

KAY. Yes. Oh, yes, Peter. *(They kiss.)*

ADDIE. *(comes in from dining room carrying a brown paper bag stuffed with her things.)* Oh. Excuse me. *(They break apart.)* I didn't mean to interrupt.

PETER. That's all right, Addie.

ADDIE. *(on the verge of tears again)* I'm leaving, Mr. Knight. I can't stay here a minute longer. *(moves above sofa)*

PETER. *(goes to her)* Now? In the middle of the night?

ADDIE. I'm afraid. You see, I know something. At least, I think I do.

PETER. What is it?

ADDIE. *(moves away L)* No, I can't tell.

KAY. Of course you can.

ADDIE. *(goes above sofa to KAY)* I always know something that could identify the killer and I never tell it.

PETER. *(to sofa L)* But you can tell this time. It's different. You're free.

ADDIE. But I've never been able to tell what I know. It's not physically possible. *(tries but fails)* You see, it's - it's - It's useless. I'll just have to run. I packed what few things I have in this paper bag. I just want to thank you, Mr. Knight and Miss Kelsey. You've both been good to me. *(starts weeping)* But I can't stay. I just can't.

KAY. Wait until morning. I beg you, Addie.

ADDIE. *(goes U C)* Storms don't bother me. I'm used to being sent out in them. Maybe this time I'll make it without getting killed.

PETER. Let me drive you to the station.

ADDIE. You can't leave. You know that. It's the rules. No, I have to go alone. Out there alone. Why does it always have to happen to me this way. *(runs out)*

PETER. Stop! Come back! *(crosses U C)*

KAY. *(goes to him)* It's no use. She has to do that.

PETER. But what if she's killed?

KAY. She probably will be.

(Off stage R there is sound of a loud crash and a scream from ADDIE which is cut short.)

PETER. My God, what was that!

KAY. *(He starts off but KAY stops him.)* You won't be able to go out the door. Let me. *(goes off up R)*

PETER. Be careful.

DICK. *(runs downstairs)* Kay. Kay, is that you?

PETER. No, it was Addie.

DICK. Gone out into the storm again, has she?

FIONA. *(comes downstairs to between PETER and DICK)* Someone else has been murdered. I knew it would happen.

DICK. Addie's left.

FIONA. *(crosses to chair L)* Good riddance.

LYDIA. *(on landing)* I heard a scream. Who was it?

PETER. *(goes above desk)* We think it was Addie.

KAY. *(comes back in slowly)* Yes, it was Addie's scream. Her last sound.

FIONA. She's dead?

KAY. Very.

DICK. *(crosses to her)* What happened?

LYDIA. *(comes downstairs and sits sofa L)* Obviously it isn't one of us. We were all upstairs.

COGBURN. *(comes onto landing)* Even me. I was turning down the beds since Addie has given her notice.

KAY. *(goes to PETER)* That large Chinese vase from the upstairs hall. It fell and smashed her head. *(goes into his arms)* It was horrible.

PETER. The vase couldn't have fallen of its own accord.

LYDIA. Hardly through a window.

FIONA. *(sits)* At precisely the right moment to kill her.

COGBURN. *(comes downstairs)* The upstairs window directly above the front door is open. Who opened it?

PETER. It must have been one of you. Tell us where you were.

FIONA. I was in my room.

DICK. *(crosses to fireplace)* I was in my room.

LYDIA. I was in my room.

COGBURN. *(by dining room exit)* I was putting a satin coverlet over the deceased. It seemed more appropriate than that crocheted afghan.

LYDIA. You were probably going through his pockets but I beat you to it.

COGBURN. I had no wish to enrich myself at your expense, Madame.

KAY. *(sinks on bench)* It's all too horrible. Another dead. Which of us will be next?

PETER. *(crosses to sofa R)* If this doesn't stop until the murderer is caught, then he or she should confess right now.

KAY. And stop more useless killings. Please, whoever you are, confess right now. *(They all exchange looks.)*

FIONA. *(knitting)* I've never been aware of a murderer confessing before he's been caught. Then he always has those long, involved speeches about how and why he did it. Mystery stories should finish with the announcement of who did it and then put "The End." That's what I'd do.

LYDIA. Which is why you're a character and not an author.

PETER. *(goes above sofa to FIONA)* Miss Babcock, you went upstairs to find your peppermints. Was that an excuse to get the Chinese vase?

FIONA. *(takes small box of peppermints from her bag)* I found the peppermints. Would you like one?

PETER. No, thank you.

FIONA. I hope everyone else has as good a reason as I have for being up there.

(knock on front door)

DICK. It's the police.

LYDIA. It can't be. Peter didn't have them in mind, did you?

PETER. No. You're all here, everyone I had thought up.

FIONA. They can't send anyone else. It's against the rules.

MINNA. *(off stage)* Hello. Peter! Mr. Knight!

PETER. It's Minna, the handyman's wife. What will I do?

KAY. Nothing. She can't see or hear us.

FIONA. Fiddlesticks, just when it was getting exciting.

MINNA. *(comes in from outside with a copy of the New York Times)* Mr. Knight - Peter - oh, there you are.

PETER. Yes, here I am.

MINNA. I didn't mean to barge right in but I knocked and didn't get any answer.

PETER. *(goes to her)* I was - er - typing and didn't hear you.

MINNA. *(hands him the Times)* I brought this morning's Times.

PETER. Thank you.

FIONA. I don't read newspapers.

PETER. *(puts paper on table L of chair L)* You didn't notice anything out front, did you?

MINNA. Out front where?

PETER. Just outside the front door. You didn't trip over anything?

MINNA. No.

LYDIA. They've taken Addie back already.

MINNA. *(goes to sofa L)* Did I miss something?

FIONA. If you only knew.

(DICK sits chair down L.)

PETER. *(by DICK at fireplace)* I just thought I left something out there.

MINNA. I was kind of nervous when you didn't answer the door. Mr. Napier, you know. He didn't answer the door when he was dead.

LYDIA. That would have been a neat trick.

PETER. I feel fine, Minna.

MINNA. *(crosses to below LYDIA)* It's the Vermont air. Keep breathin' it.

LYDIA. You got that, Peter? Keep breathing.

MINNA. Mind if I sit a spell?

PETER. Not at all.

(MINNA goes to sit on LYDIA.)

LYDIA. No. Not on me.

FIONA. *(rises leaving her knitting in chair)* Quick. Over here. *(moves above her chair)*

PETER. *(pushes MINNA to chair L)* Not there. This is more comfortable.

MINNA. If you say so. *(picks up knitting)* What is this thing?

FIONA. Don't pull my needles out.

PETER. It's knitting.

MINNA. *(sits)* You do this?

PETER. Occupational therapy. It relaxes me.

MINNA. *(turning it around)* Which way is up?

FIONA. *(points)* That's the top.

PETER. *(points)* That's the top.

MINNA. What's it goin' to be, a tea cozy?

FIONA. No.

PETER. No.

MINNA. What then?

PETER. Well - *(looks to FIONA who gives a gesture of helplessness)*

MINNA. I reckon it's to cover somethin'.

PETER. My typewriter.

FIONA. Well, really.

PETER. *(takes knitting)* So it won't get dusty.

(FIONA grabs it and puts it on table beside chair. MINNA does not see this.)

MINNA. Well, everyone to his own taste as the old lady said when she kissed the cow.

LYDIA. That is the most revolting thing I have ever heard.

PETER. You said that before.

MINNA. I know. It's an expression fits in most anywhere. How's your mystery comin'?

PETER. I've been stuck for awhile.

MINNA. Any murders yet?

PETER. One.

FIONA. Two.

PETER. Two.

LYDIA. And you might be number three.

MINNA. Then you're makin' progress.

DICK. Say, maybe she knows where the bonds are hidden.

PETER. *(to DICK)* Maybe she does.

MINNA. Who?

PETER. You.

MINNA. Maybe I do what?

PETER. Maybe you do know some hiding place in here.

MINNA. For what?

PETER. *(sits on L sofa arm leaning towards her)* In my book I want a hiding place for some papers.

KAY. You're so clever.

PETER. And I thought if there was a real place I wouldn't have to make one up.

MINNA. Well - *(closes her eyes and thinks)*

FIONA. *(leans over L of chair looking down at her)* Is she dead or thinking?

COGBURN. I think she's dead.

MINNA. *(snaps to)* Nope.

LYDIA. She lives.

MINNA. Don't know of no such thing as a hidin' place hereabouts. I got one though. You twist off the top ball on my brass bed and there's a big hollar place underneath. You can use that if you want to.

FIONA. What's she keep there, her grandmother's silver?

MINNA. That's where I keep my grandmother's silver.

LYDIA. Bingo! *(They all laugh and PETER joins in.)*

MINNA. What's so funny? I got three forks and six knives in there and one teaspoon from the Chicago World's Fair.

PETER. I wasn't laughing at that, Minna. It was something else.

MINNA. *(rises)* Well, this place is no laughing matter. My pigs keep their sty better'n this. *(goes below sofa to desk)* Don't you ever wash up?

PETER. I was just going to.

MINNA. Lands sakes, you'll have every fly in Vermont in here. *(starts collecting glasses from desk)*

PETER. *(goes to her)* I'll clear them up.

LYDIA. She doesn't mind.

MINNA. I don't mind.

COGBURN. But I do.

MINNA. *(holds up the bud vase)* You been drinkin' out of this here vase?

PETER. I thought it was a beer stein.

MINNA. This here's for a single flower.

COGBURN. I would prefer she didn't set foot in my kitchen.

PETER. *(follows MINNA as she gets cups and glasses from table above sofa)* You're not paid to do this, Minna. Please let me.

MINNA. *(gets FIONA'S cup from table L, puts them all on tray above sofa)* You menfolk need tendin' to.

KAY. Oh, yes. I agree.

MINNA. That's the lot of 'em. *(exits through dining room)*

COGBURN. Oh, sir, don't let her wash them. I have my own system.

PETER. She seems very determined. *(as he follows her off)* Just leave them, Minna. Wait till I have a machine full.

COGBURN. *(follows him off)* I hope she doesn't find the Chivas Regal.

LYDIA. That one is the original eager beaver.

FIONA. Cleanliness is next to Godliness.

KAY. I keep my place neat as a pin.

DICK. I-

LYDIA. I know. You believe her.

DICK. That's exactly what I was going to say.

PETER. *(off stage)* Thank you so much, Minna.

MINNA. *(enters, crosses above sofa and straightens magazines ... PETER follows her.)* I'd wash up but I wouldn't tackle one of them new-fangled washin' machines.

COGBURN. *(enters)* She didn't touch the Chivas.

PETER. I'll do them after supper.

MINNA. *(eagerly)* You want me to stay and cook somethin' for you?

LYDIA. No.

FIONA. No.

DICK. No.

KAY. No.

COGBURN. Definitely not.

PETER. I think not. I have a frozen Hawaiian dinner.

MINNA. The Bicarb's over the sink.

PETER. *(takes her U C)* Thanks for bringing the paper. Isn't midnight past your bedtime?

MINNA. You think it's past midnight?

KAY. Time is different for her.

PETER. I got to writing and didn't notice. Is it early?

MINNA. *(goes to sofa via R side and plumps pillows)* Shank of the evening.

LYDIA. *(rises and circles MINNA as she does the pillows)* Oh, go home and milk the cows.

PETER. That's all right, Minna. I'll straighten up tomorrow.

MINNA. Ayah, if you say so.

PETER. Everything may be cleared up by then.

MINNA. *(crosses to PETER and LYDIA resits on sofa)* What needs clearin' up?

PETER. The weather.

KAY. Such quick thinking.

MINNA. Why it's as clear as the stare of a glass eye.

FIONA. How repulsive. *(sits in chair L)*

PETER. I thought it was raining.

MINNA. T'ain't.

PETER. Running water, that's what it was. I forgot to jiggle the toilet handle.

MINNA. You sure you don't want me to stay with you for awhile? You're soundin' lonely.

PETER. No, no, I'm fine.

MINNA. You sure you ain't been swiggin' a bit too much?

PETER. I haven't drunk a thing.

MINNA. But all them glasses?

FIONA. Explain them if you can.

PETER. *(moves below bench)* It's for my story. I've been acting it out.

KAY. He's so clever.

MINNA. *(goes to PETER)* My Uncle Buttram used to act things out with imaginary folk before they hauled him off.

PETER. He's cured now?

MINNA. They stopped him drinkin' all right, but my Aunt Cora said sober he was downright ornery so she likkered him up again and they're celebratin' their forty-ninth anniversary come Saturday.

LYDIA. If Uncle Buttram is sober enough.

MINNA. Well, I'm off. I won't forget to pick up your Phil Smith on the mornin' bus. *(goes U C)*

PETER. *(crosses to her)* Thanks, Minna. *(He takes her off to front door.)*

FIONA. *(takes peppermints from bag)* Now perhaps we can get on with it.

LYDIA. There was a pair of Chinese vases upstairs. Maybe she'll get the other one.

COGBURN. No, she's a real person.

KAY. So is Peter and someone tried to kill him.

PETER. *(comes back in)* She didn't see Addie's body.

COGBURN. It's gone, sir.

DICK. They've taken her back.

KAY. I hope she gets a happier assignment next time.

FIONA. She's a wanton girl and she always will be. *(starts to eat a peppermint)*

PETER. Don't touch that!

FIONA. What? My peppermint?

PETER. They were up in your room?

FIONA. Yes, I'd left them there.

FIONA. You're right. It is about time I was murdered. But they look so tasty.

KAY. *(rises and goes to sofa L)* I'll eat one to test them.

PETER. No.

KAY. *(takes a mint and crosses to fireplace)* They never kill the ingenue. It's not cricket.

DICK. *(rises)* We're free; this isn't like other stories.

COGBURN. He has a point, Miss.

KAY. I'll chance it.

DICK. *(grabs it from her)* Let me. If you think they won't kill the ingenue, then they won't kill the juvenile either. Let's see. *(He eats it. They all watch him.)*

PETER. You were right.

DICK. No, I was wrong. *(gasps and drops dead)*

KAY. Dick! *(PETER leans over him.)*

COGBURN. Mr. Stanton!

FIONA. My peppermint!

LYDIA. Three down and five to go.

KAY. What does it all mean?

PETER. If someone is trying to kill not only the author but the ingenue and juvenile as well, we're all in danger.

KAY. But who could it be?

PETER. Someone in this room.

CURTAIN

ACT TWO

Scene 2

(A short time later. There is a tray on the table above sofa. Thay are all eating sandwiches and drinking coffee. PETER sits in desk chair, FIONA on the bench, KAY on the sofa and LYDIA in chair L.)

LYDIA. When you haven't eaten in years anything is gourmet.

KAY. It feels so good to really chew on something. Usually we don't get real food, just make-believe.

FIONA. What is this filling?

PETER. It's called Spam.

LYDIA. I'd give anything for a good roast beef.

PETER. We couldn't chance that. This way, with all of us watching Cogburn open the can we know it hadn't been tampered with.

FIONA. I prefer tea myself, but this coffee isn't bad.

PETER. It's instant.

FIONA. What will they think of next?

KAY. *(rises and puts plate on table above sofa, picks up her coffee cup)* What will we think of next? There are only five of us left and one of us is a murderer.

PETER. It obviously isn't me because my drink was poisoned.

LYDIA. Yes, but you didn't drink it, darling. Perhaps you put the cyanide into your own drink to fool us.

PETER. And it isn't Kay because she's the only link to the bearer bonds. No one can kill her until the bonds are found.

FIONA. Unless Kay really knows where they are. Then she can kill all of us and escape.

KAY. *(crosses to FIONA)* But I was here in the room when the vase fell on Addie.

LYDIA. *(rises and puts her plate on table above sofa)* That's a perfect alibi but I've seen perfect alibis destroyed before.

KAY. Then how would I have dropped the vase?

LYDIA. I don't know. I'm not the murderer.

KAY. Aren't you?

LYDIA. *(picks up her coffee from table L)* Maybe there was a wire from the vase to the front door handle and when Addie opened the door it pulled the vase down on her.

PETER. It's obvious you aren't a writer.

LYDIA. And it's obvious you're not a very good one or we wouldn't be in this pickle.

PETER. *(rises)* I didn't ask you to come here.

LYDIA. *(moves below sofa)* Yes you did. What kind of an author would get a lot of characters down on paper without knowing what was going to happen?

PETER. That's the way I work.

LYDIA. *(sits on sofa)* Then it's a lousy way.

FIONA. I am in total accord.

KAY. *(Stopping the building fight, she crosses above sofa to L.)* Please, lets not bicker. That won't get us anywhere.

PETER. *(goes to table above sofa)* You're right, of course.

LYDIA. My odds-on favorite for the murderer is Fiona Babcock.

FIONA. Tommyrot.

LYDIA. She's one of those moral fanatics who disapproves of everyone else. She was upstairs when the vase fell on Addie, she even had the poisoned peppermints in her possesion. Yes, my favorite is you, Fiona.

FIONA. *(rises)* And my favorite is you. Everyone knows I'm not a murderer. I get murdered. Always. I've been poisoned with a hypodermic needle, hung in a barn, drowned in the surf at Carmel, but I have never committed murder. I don't approve of it. *(crosses to chair L)*

KAY. But you're free now.

FIONA. We have to keep in character, don't we? Have any of you been able to make a complete change? No.

LYDIA. But wouldn't it be rational for your character to kill us, get the bonds and use the money for some good cause?

FIONA. *(thinks a moment)* You know, you're right. I could be the murderer. *(sits in chair and picks up knitting)* But I'm not.

PETER. *(crosses to dining room)* There's one person we're forgetting.

KAY. Of course. Cogburn.

LYDIA. But he's a butler. He always has been and he always will be. He wouldn't know how to behave in the outside world. He is an appendage to another person. He can't operate unless his room and board are provided and he has his duties. No, Cogburn is out.

KAY. *(goes to sofa R)* We must be wrong somewhere.

PETER. About what?

KAY. *(sits on bench)* About one of us. It has got to be one of us.

LYDIA. There is another thing we've overlooked.

PETER. What's that?

LYDIA. A person we think has already been murdered.

KAY. Your husband? But he's dead. We all saw him dead.

FIONA. She's right. Agatha Christie did that once. We all think someone is dead and he isn't and -

LYDIA. So he has the run of the house without our suspecting him.

KAY. Then it could even be Dick?

FIONA. Most ingenious. The juvenile gets murdered, which is quite unheard of, and then turns out to be the actual killer.

PETER. It's simple enough to go upstairs and see if Dick and Jordan are still dead. *(crosses to foot of stairs)*

KAY. They might have been taken back for another assignment.

PETER. You mean like Addie? Her body disappeared right away.

FIONA. She might be on another job but I doubt it. Her type is a dime a dozen. It's the few character women like me who are always in demand.

LYDIA. *(rises and goes to FIONA)* I'll have you know that I have been working steadily on fifteen stories non-stop, and I might add I always see you hanging around the waiting room with your eternal knitting when I pass through.

FIONA. I only appear in the better stories. Your type of high-class golddigger is in every first novel. I bet you never get a return appearance with the same author.

LYDIA. *(goes to fireplace)* I wish I had my resume with me.

FIONA. And I wish I had my book reviews.

PETER. *(moves down above sofa)* Will you stop it? Why don't you bury the hatchet and agree you're both good at what you do? Fiona, I think you are a perfect self-righteous spinster. Absolutely perfect.

FIONA. Thank you.

PETER. And Lydia, there is no one more attractive, worldly, and sensual than you.

LYDIA. No one?

PETER. Not one single person. You are both perfect for what I wanted. That's why I thought you up the way you are.

KAY. Isn't it nice of Peter? Now, why don't you shake hands and be friends?

LYDIA. We're not prize-fighters meeting in the ring.

FIONA. I am willing to concede that Lydia does what she does very well. I just don't approve of her doing it.

LYDIA. And I concede that Fiona doesn't do anything right but she does it beautifully.

FIONA. Thank you.

KAY. You may never be friends but there's no need to be enemies.

PETER. *(goes up to landing)* Now I'll go and see if Dick and Mr. Dillingham are still there. Suppose they're not, how will we know if they're roaming the house or if they've been called back?

LYDIA. *(goes up L)* They don't get called back unless they're dead and then all their props go with them.

FIONA. If their personal belongings are gone, they're killed dead.

KAY. *(to foot of stairs)* Be careful, Peter.

FIONA. I, for one, wouldn't go up there while one of us is not accounted for.

LYDIA. Cogburn. I'll call him. *(pulls the bell rope)* Fiona, that was a genius idea of yours.

FIONA. *(sweetly)* Thank you. It's very kind of you to say so.

LYDIA. *(just as sweetly)* Not at all. *(crosses and sits in chair down L)*

KAY. *(goes above sofa)* It's so much nicer when you two get along. It gives off a glow.

PETER. Where is Cogburn?

LYDIA. He must have heard the bell.

FIONA. Dead. I know he's been murdered.

KAY. He couldn't be. We're all in here.

FIONA. Booby trap, like the vase and Addie.

LYDIA. A short circuit in his Cuisinart.

FIONA. A loosened step on the cellar stairs.

LYDIA. The gas left on in the oven.

FIONA. Ground glass in his vitamin pill.

KAY. Stop it! Stop it! Both of you. He can't be dead. He's too nice a man.

FIONA. You would think so.

KAY. *(runs toward dining room)* Cogburn! Cogburn!

COGBURN. *(catches her as he enters calmly)* Yes, Miss.

KAY. You're not dead?

COGBURN. On the contrary.

PETER. We thought something had happened to you.

COGBURN. I was repairing a loose step on the cellar stairs.

FIONA. I was right.

COGBURN. You rang?

LYDIA. I did.

COGBURN. What did you wish, Madame?

LYDIA. *(thinking quickly)* Some hot coffee, please.

COGBURN. Certainly, Madame. You can go upstairs now, Mr. Knight.

PETER. How did you - ?

COGBURN. Naturally, I assume you called me in here so you could keep an eye on me while one of you left the room. Since you are on the landing, I conclude it is you who wishes to depart.

PETER. Very clever of you, Cogburn.

COGBURN. Thank you, sir. And you will remember to jiggle the handle?

PETER. Yes, thank you. *(He goes off. KAY sits on bench.)*

COGBURN. Do you really wish more coffee, Madame?

LYDIA. No, it was just an excuse.

COGBURN. *(after a pause)* I assume neither the bonds nor the murderer has been found or there wouldn't be such gloom in here.

KAY. You're right. We have gotten nowhere.

COGBURN. Perhaps this will be the one completely unsolved mystery ever written.

LYDIA. That wouldn't be sporting.

FIONA. We must find the murderer.

KAY. And the bonds.

LYDIA. You can't finish a story without all the loose ends being tied up.

COGBURN. But since we are free, perhaps it won't finish.

FIONA. I'm not going back until I know who it is.

COGBURN. We may have no choice. As we are killed off, we return. It will be a feather in our caps, as it were, to be involved in the only perfect murder ever written. Quite an addition to our resumes.

PETER. *(comes downstairs and goes to KAY)* It's not either of them.

LYDIA. The bodies have disappeared?

PETER. Not a trace of them.

COGBURN. And their belongings, sir?

PETER. Gone, too.

COGBURN. *(crosses to tray above sofa)* Then we know it isn't someone wandering around the place. The killer is definitely a person in this room.

PETER. It appears that way.

COGBURN. How interesting. *(exits with tray)*

KAY. I hope he doesn't drown in the dishwasher.

LYDIA. Since we're all here it wouldn't be murder, it would be suicide.

FIONA. Now what? We can't all stay here in this room watching each other for the rest of our - what shall I call it? - allowed time.

KAY. But Peter isn't like the rest of us. If he's killed, he'll be dead like Norman Napier was.

LYDIA. *(rises and goes below sofa)* Poor Peter. No other assignments for you. Just eternity.

PETER. *(goes above desk)* I'm trying to avoid it.

LYDIA. *(after a pause)* There are four of us. Do we all play bridge?

FIONA. I never touch cards.

LYDIA. *(sits on sofa)* I should have known. Not that I mind, Fiona, dear. To each his own.

PETER. *(crosses R of desk and sits)* Let's start back at the beginning again.

LYDIA. When you first called us here?

PETER. No, at the bonds. If we find them, the murderer will have to make a play for them.

KAY. *(rises)* I've been thinking until I have a headache.

FIONA. *(Fishing in her bag, she comes out with a bottle of aspirin.)* Would you like an aspirin, dear?

KAY. Thank you, I'd appreciate that. *(starts for it)*

PETER. *(rises)* Kay, no!

LYDIA. They might be stronger than you want.

KAY. My headache's suddenly gone. Just like that.

FIONA. *(puts aspirin bottle back)* You're right not to trust anyone.

KAY. *(sits on sofa with LYDIA)* There's nothing I can think of that will help find the bonds, Peter.

PETER. Let's recreate the scene then. You were three years old.

KAY. We had a wonderful dinner, Mr Humberton and I. We ended up with ice cream and little cookies shaped like Christmas trees. He was always so kind to me after my parents died. If he hadn't picked me out of the orphanage, I don't know what would have happened to me.

PETER. *(goes above desk)* Go on. And then?

KAY. *(rises and indicates chair L)* We came in here and sat in front of the fire.

PETER. And he read A CHRISTMAS CAROL to you.

KAY. That's what I remember. I don't recall too much of the story because I fell asleep.

FIONA. You were drugged.

KAY. What reason would he have to do that?

LYDIA. I can think of plenty.

FIONA. A pretty young girl with an old lecherous man?

KAY. *(crosses to fireplace)* That's a horrible thing to say about him. He was kindness itself.

PETER. *(goes above sofa)* So you went to sleep while he was reading to you. Then what?

KAY. I awoke as the clock was striking midnight. It was Christmas Day and the most wonderful thing had happened.

LYDIA. You saw him put the bonds somewhere?

KAY. No, there was a huge Christmas tree standing right over there. *(points down R)* It had decorations and candy canes on it. It was like magic. *(goes below sofa to bench)* And there, underneath, were presents, everything a child could wish for. Toys, dolls, clothes, everything.

PETER. *(to her R)* What did you do?

KAY. I remember looking up at Mr. Humberton. I asked him what had happened. He smiled and said, "Santa Claus has been here." I could see tears in his eyes behind his bi-focals. *(sits on bench)*

PETER. Then what?

KAY. I told him I would remember that moment the rest of my life. I opened my presents and then I went to bed the happiest little girl in the world.

FIONA. Sentimental twaddle.

LYDIA. There's no clue in that.

KAY. That's what I said.

PETER. *(sits R sofa arm facing front)* But there is. There must be. Let's see, now, something happened there that Mr. Humberton thought you would remember over all these years.

KAY. Yes, but what?

PETER. We must think. Let me say a word and you answer with the first thing that comes into your head.

FIONA. I loathe games.

LYDIA. The next thing we know you'll have her reading ink blots.

PETER. Just give us a chance, will you? *(rises)* Ready?

KAY. Yes.

PETER. Humberton.

KAY. Kind.

PETER. *(crosses above sofa and turns to her suddenly)* Christmas.

KAY. Happy.

PETER. Christmas here.

KAY. Santa Claus.

PETER. That's it!

KAY. What?

PETER. Santa Claus.

LYDIA. What's he got to do with it?

PETER. You told Mr. Humberton you would remember the moment of Santa Claus having come the rest of your life.

KAY. That's right.

PETER. He remembered that and hoped you would.

KAY. But how does that help?

PETER. Where does Santa Claus come from?

KAY. Down the chimney, but - *(rises)* Is that it?

PETER. The chimney! *(crosses to fireplace KAY follows and FIONA rises.)*

LYDIA. *(crosses to fireplace after the others)* I don't believe this.

FIONA. Fairy tales always have pots of gold at the end of the rainbow but never up a chimney.

KAY. *(to PETER who has his hand up the chimney)* Is anything there?

PETER. I can't seem to - wait a minute - there's something. It's metal. *(A metal box falls down along with some soot.)* There!

KAY. Peter, is that it? *(PETER puts the box on chair down L.)*

LYDIA. *(Now she is excited.)* I now believe in Santa Claus.

FIONA. Open it. I can't take the suspense.

PETER. I'm trying to get it open.

KAY. Won't the bonds be burnt?

PETER. *(opens lid of box)* It's lined in asbestos and - here it is - an envelope. *(pulls out an oil-skin wrapped envelope, goes below sofa)*

KAY. *(follows him)* Peter, you found it.

LYDIA. *(moves above sofa)* Can we order champagne?

FIONA. *(crosses to L of sofa)* To celebrate this, even I would take a drink.

PETER. *(has opened envelope and holds up bonds)* Here they are. *(sits back on sofa triumphantly)*

LYDIA. They're very small for such a large fortune.

FIONA. May I touch them?

PETER. It's up to Kay. They're hers. Here you are, Miss Kelsey. *(hands bonds to her)*

KAY. *(moves R of sofa looking where Christmas tree was)* How generous of Mr. Humberton and I do thank him, but what good are they to me? If I leave here I won't know how to behave in the outside world without someone writing what I do.

LYDIA. *(crosses to her)* I'd know how to behave. I'll take them.

KAY. Perhaps some charity would be glad to receive them.

FIONA. *(laughs)* Ironic, isn't it? The ingenue gets the fortune and it doesn't do anyone any good.

KAY. *(sits bench)* But if it's mine and I am killed then it will disappear along with me won't it?

PETER. *(rises)* Then we must see you don't get killed.

LYDIA. *(crosses to PETER)* You might include the rest of us.

PETER. *(goes to fireplace)* The murderer must have made a slip. They always do.

FIONA. *(goes below chair L)* This might be the exception that proves the rule.

PETER. Jordan and Dick were both poisoned. It's not likely we'll find a clue connected with that. But the vase that killed Addie, that's another matter. That's tangible. *(to L of sofa)* I'm going up and reconstruct that crime; find out exactly how it was done.

LYDIA. *(goes to fireplace)* What could be simpler than to drop a vase on a head?

(FIONA sits in chair L.)

PETER. *(at foot of stairs)* But there might be something overlooked that will point to one of us.

KAY. Peter. *(rises)*

PETER. Yes.

KAY. Don't go up there until -

PETER. Until what?

COGBURN. *(appears around dining room arch)* Until you have called Cogburn.

LYDIA. You were listening.

COGBURN. It's a butler's perogative.

PETER. You heard about the bonds?

COGBURN. Yes. *(to KAY)* Congratulations, Miss.

KAY. Thank you.

COGBURN. I hold no ill. I wish I could speak for the rest in this room.

PETER. You will stay here while I'm upstairs, won't you?

COGBURN. If you wish, sir.

PETER. I wish. *(on landing)* I'm going to check that window.

COGBURN. If you would be so good, sir -

PETER. Yes?

COGBURN. *(moves into below landing)* After you've finished, it would spare me a trip upstairs if you would turn the switch behind the left drape to "ON". It's the burglar alarm.

PETER. Just for that one window?

COGBURN. Mr. Humberton had seperate ones installed in all the hall windows.

PETER. *(starts off)* Very well. I'll turn the - *(turns)* Cogburn.

COGBURN. Yes, sir.

PETER. How did you know the switch was off?

COGBURN. If the window is open it must be.

PETER. You said it's behind a drape. No one could have seen it and only you knew about it.

KAY. Oh, no!

LYDIA. *(rises)* Cogburn!

COGBURN. I made a fatal slip, didn't I?

PETER. *(comes downstairs)* Murderers in stories always do.

FIONA. Never trust servants, that's my motto.

PETER. You put poison in my drink when the lights failed, then you must have goaded poor Addie into leaving knowing you could get upstairs and drop the Chinese vase on her.

FIONA. *(rises)* Then you put cyanide in my peppermints.

KAY. *(moves down to bench)* But you killed poor Dick instead.

COGBURN. *(goes to sofa L)* I didn't care which of you got it.

PETER. *(goes by KAY)* But why, Cogburn? Why would you do this?

COGBURN. To get back my reputation.

LYDIA. But you have an excellent reputation.

COGBURN. Not only as a butler but as a murderer.

KAY. You want to be known as a murderer?

COGBURN. *(goes below sofa)* What have we butlers become? Merely men who serve and demean ourselves. We're not important, we're not interesting. We're nothing. But in the old days - ah, we had respect, we had recognition. *(goes to PETER)* It's all your fault, you and the other authors. You never use us properly any more.

We've become a laughing stock. Does anyone ever say that immortal line any more?

PETER. What immortal line?

COGBURN. "The butler did it!"

(FIONA sits in chair L.)

PETER. So that's what upset you?

COGBURN. It became so trite. *(crosses away L)* But this butler has brought back esteem to all butlers. I'm glad I did it.

KAY. *(crosses to him)* And we thought it was someone after these bonds.

COGBURN. Oh, I wanted those, too.

KAY. Why?

COGBURN. Once I had killed all of you, especially Mr. Knight, then I would be free.

LYDIA. *(sits down L)* You'd never make it in the real world.

COGBURN. I'm not like Rodney Durston. He was a fool.

PETER. Who is Rodney Durston?

LYDIA. He used to be on call for small-time crooks. Hasn't been around lately.

FIONA. That's right. I haven't seen him in eons.

COGBURN. He's the one who killed Norman Napier.

PETER. *(goes to R of desk)* Right here at his typewriter?

COGBURN. An overdose of Demoral gives the appearance of a heart attack.

KAY. *(sits on sofa)* Durston did that?

COGBURN. That's the last time anyone was free like we

are. But Durston headed out into the world without any real money and no knowledge. He couldn't cope and he threw himself off the Eiffel Tower and sent himself back.

FIONA. Suicide. They'll never forgive him for that.

COGBURN. He now works for authors of cartoons and is on television early Saturday mornings.

LYDIA. How terrible.

FIONA. The ultimate disgrace.

COGBURN. *(goes to sofa R)* But I'm not like that. I know the best clothes, the best vintage wines, the correct way to live. *(goes to sofa L)* I've been taught by the greatest authors. The world was going to be mine, and it still will be. *(He pulls pistol from his pocket, grabs KAY and pulls her in front of him with the gun to her head. She screams as he pulls her to the L of the sofa.)*

KAY. No, don't!

PETER. *(starts below desk)* Let her go!

FIONA. *(rises)* Someone stop him!

COGBURN. *(to PETER)* One step closer and I'll blow her head off.

KAY. Take the bonds. I don't want them.

COGBURN. I'll take them all right. *(puts them in his pocket)* The first thing I'll do is to hire a butler of my own. Now to get rid of our author so I'll stay free.

KAY. No, it's not fair.

LYDIA. You'll be killing the hand that types us.

PETER. Then I'll be with you, Kay.

KAY. No, you're real and we're not. We can never be together.

FIONA. *(searching in her knitting bag)* There's only one way to stop you.

COGBURN. *(his eyes always on PETER)* There is no way.

FIONA. Oh, yes, there is. *(pulls pistol from bag)* I can kill you.

LYDIA. Fiona Babcock!

COGBURN. I'll shoot Kay first.

FIONA. And I'll get you. If we all die, we'll all be sent back and you'll end up with Durston doing cartoons.

COGBURN. Not if I kill Knight first.

FIONA. The moment you turn that gun towards him you're dead. *(They are at a stand-off, COGBURN with his gun to KAY'S head and FIONA with her gun on him.)* I must say this is rather exciting.

LYDIA. Fiona, this is so unlike you.

FIONA. Since I'm free, I took this gun from your husband's suitcase before they took him back. I thought I'd see how it felt to be behind a gun for a change. It is most exhilarating.

LYDIA. We seem to be at a stand-off.

KAY. You can save us, Peter.

PETER. There's nothing I can do.

KAY. Yes, there is. Finish the story. It doesn't matter what it is as long as it is finished. Then we'll all go back.

COGBURN. No, you can't do that!

KAY. Please, Peter.

LYDIA. I'm afraid it is the only way.

FIONA. I do want to return to my little cottage.

COGBURN. *(to PETER)* I'll shoot you first.

KAY. *(As COGBURN turns the gun towards PETER, she knocks it out of his hand.)* No, you don't! *(kicks pistol under sofa)*

LYDIA. Shoot, Fiona.

FIONA. I can't do it! It's out of character.

PETER. *(rushes to typewriter)* I'll finish the story.

COGBURN. *(starts for PETER during above...KAY trips him and he goes down on the floor.)* I'll stop him.

PETER. *(types)* T - h - e   E - n - d.

COGBURN. *(During above, gets to his feet and starts toward PETER.)* No!

KAY. Good bye, Peter.

(As he finishes typing, blackout with lightning flash. During the blackout, KAY, LYDIA, COGBURN, and FIONA, with her knitting, exit.)

PETER. *(goes above desk)* I finished it! I wrote "The End". Where are you? Have you gone? Kay - Kay - The flashlight? I can't find it. Kay - Kay - *(Lights up to morning brightness.)* *(He looks around and finds himself alone.)* Where have you -? *(crosses up C)* A dream? Was it a dream? *(comes down to sofa L)* No, they were here. All of them. The bonds? Fiona's knitting? *(looks for it in chair L)* Have I gone crazy? *(Knock on front door. PETER starts for door, looks back at room.)* You were here, weren't you? I know you were here. *(goes off to front door)*

MINNA. *(off stage)* It's a beautiful morning, isn't it, Mr. Knight? *(She comes in followed by PETER.)* Leave the door open and get some of that good sunlight into the place.

PETER. It's morning?

MINNA. *(by sofa L)* Tain't nighttime when the sun's out.

PETER. *(to sofa L)* But what time is it?

MINNA. About forty-five after eleven. You look terrible. Did you sleep well?

PETER. *(still in a daze)* No, I was working, all night it seems.

MINNA. Sorry I'm not bringin' you any help but that Phil Smith never got off the bus.

PETER. He didn't?

MINNA. *(sits bench)* Nope. Now you won't have anyone to take your dictation or anythin', will you?

PETER. I guess not.

KAY. *(off stage)* Hello. Anyone home?

PETER. *(startled)* Kay. Kay, is that you? *(crosses below landing)*

(KAY comes into archway. She has changed from the KAY we knew. She is in a different dress and carries a suitcase and a purse.)

KAY. No. Sorry if you're expecting a Kay. How do you do. I'm Phil Smith. *(crosses to PETER and offers her hand)*

MINNA. *(rises)* You ain't a man?

KAY. *(smiles and puts her suitcase down)* Hardly. Oh, of course you're confused. I'm Phyllis Smith, but everyone calls me Phil.

MINNA. I'm Minna.

KAY. *(crosses to sofa L)* Glad to meet you, Minna.

PETER. *(comes down above sofa)* Haven't we met before?

KAY. I don't think so.

MINNA. That's an old line.

PETER. I mean it.

MINNA. *(goes U C)* Well, I'm off to the farm. Gotta spread some manure. Glad you're here to help. *(exits U C)*

KAY. Thank goodness there was a taxi of sorts to meet the bus.

PETER. *(still in shock)* I sent Minna there but she was looking for a man.

KAY. *(looking over the room, crosses to fireplace)* Your agent should have said I was a girl.

PETER. *(by sofa L)* Alan Jupiter is very vague until it comes to his percentage.

KAY. *(crosses below sofa)* Say, this is a wonderful, gloomy old place, isn't it?

PETER. That it is.

KAY. *(crosses to bench while pointing to R)* Wouldn't it be marvelous to have Christmas here? I'd put the tree there and *(indicates chair L)* I'd sit there in front of the fire and read A CHRISTMAS CAROL and wait for Santa Claus. Wouldn't you?

PETER. *(crosses below sofa)* Yes. Yes, I would.

KAY. What kind of a typewriter do you have? *(goes to it)* Looks fine. Let's try it out. *(sits, moving chair to typewriter)* It says "The End". Have you finished?

PETER. *(moves above desk)* No, that was just where I'd stopped typing.

KAY. You're not a very good typist, are you? It's all gone funny here with odd letters. Let's start back at the top of the page. You left off with - *(reads)* "Oblivious of the storm's warning, Lydia comes to the top of the stairs." *(LYDIA does. Now PETER cannot see or hear her.)* "She is an exquisite creature. Lydia is probably forty-two years old.

But she carries it well and only a close inspection would tell her true age, and many men have had the advantage of that close inspection."

LYDIA. Here we go again.

KAY. "As usual, she is dressed with impeccable taste. A green scarf is wound round her throat."

LYDIA. Oh, not again, Peter, please.

PETER. No. No, Phil. Change that to a blue scarf. *(looks front and smiles)* Yes, blue is Lydia's color.

LYDIA. Peter, you angel. *(rushes back off the landing to exit)*

KAY. Blue scarf. Go on.

PETER. See how this sounds. *(KAY types as PETER talks slowly. He crosses down to just above her chair.)* She comes down the stairs to meet Kay who is a beautiful girl. *(lights dim during the following)* She brought a breath of spring into the gloomy old house. Her presence makes everyone feel alive. In fact, she is every man's dream of who he wants to spend the rest of his life with ... *(lights have dimmed to black)*

CURTAIN

PROPERTY LIST

ACT ONE

On Stage:
> Typewriter with sheet half typed in it on typing table
> Magazines including READER'S DIGEST and NEWSWEEK on table above sofa
> Pads, pencils, pens, paper on desk
> Flashlight in desk drawer

Off Up Left *(Upstairs)*:
> Green scarf *(LYDIA)*
> Knitting bag with half-knitted multi-colored garment, needles and wool *(FIONA)*
> Handkerchief *(ADDIE)*
> Folded will in large envelope with seal *(JORDAN)*

Off Left *(Dining Room)*:
> Tray with two highballs *(COGBURN)*
> Tray with tea cup, saucer, sugar bowl, cream pitcher, spoon *(COGBURN)*
> Tray with single cup of tea *(COGBURN)*
> Tray with six assorted glasses including bud vase, jelly glass, etc. all partially filled *(ADDIE)*

Off Up Right *(Outside)*:
> Suitcase *(KAY)*
> Suitcase *(DICK)*

PROPERTY LIST

ACT TWO

SCENE 1.
  Off Up Left *(Upstairs)*:
    Small box of peppermints *(FIONA)*

  Off Left *(Dining Room)*:
    Brown paper bag, stuffed *(ADDIE)*

  Off Up Right *(Outside)*:
    New York Times *(MINNA)*

SCENE 2.

  On Stage:
    Small metal box, asbestos-lined, containing oil
      skin covered envelope with bonds in it
    Bottle of aspirin, pistol in knitting bag *(FIONA)*
    Plates of sandwiches and coffee cups on desk
      (PETER), bench *(FIONA)*, sofa *(KAY)*, and
      chair L *(LYDIA)*

  Off Up Left *(Upstairs)*:
    Blue scarf *(LYDIA)*

  Off Left *(Dining Room)*:
    Pistol *(COGBURN)*

  Off Up Right *(Outside)*:
    Suitcase *(KAY)*

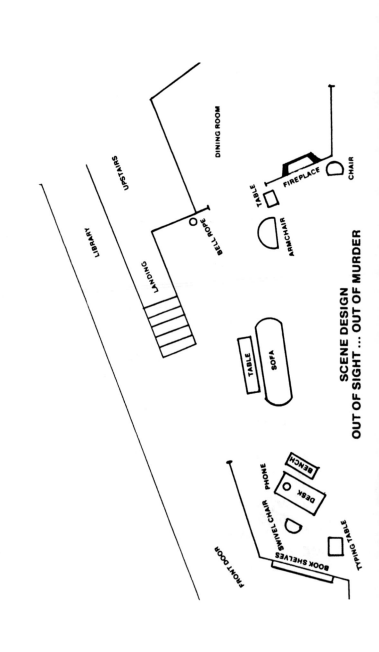

SCENE DESIGN
OUT OF SIGHT ... OUT OF MURDER

SAMUELFRENCH.COM

CPSIA information can be obtained at www.ICGtesting.com
Printed in the USA
BVOW07s0602250913

332109BV00011B/775/P